Published by Cacti-Knights

ISBN: 978-1-63041-011-7
First edition: 18th May 2014
Copyright ©2014 by Cacti-Knights

Nurielm

Tales from the Etheric

For
Riley, Laine, Luke, and Jagan

"Curiosity is insubordination in its purest form"
Vladimir Nabokov

Contents

Preface 3
GM-Oh Dear 4
A Dark Honour 21
Ascenders 22... 26
Entity Tea Time Transformation 57
Jasper, the Relationship Ghoul 61
Holistic Revolution Flip 74
Souls Waiting Room.. 104
The Ever Increasing Empath 118
Earth Splitz Reset... 152
Galactic Butterflies 170

Preface

The structures and messages within each story were gained in altered states of consciousness, and I didn't know it at the time, but this was just the beginning.

It's pretty crazy what I went through to actually 'develop' these stories, in more ways than one.   In a personal-life sense, I became sort of synchronistically linked to some of the stories, wherein some of the forces and emotions I was writing about actually started to weave into my life and play through me.   This I feel was so I could write about them better, or at least understand them better, as when they were written, that emotion or force would leave my life and the next one on the menu would come in.

Some of the stories contain darkness, but as any true adept, searcher, or scholar knows, darkness is not to be negated, but to be understood, known, and brought out into the light.....and hey, the human species on (the beautiful and harmonic) earth is in a dark place at the moment, and at a pivotal moment.

I hope you find some enjoyment in a tale or two from this humble collection.

mark

GM-Oh Dear

Jonnie at twenty-seven felt in his prime, he had the brains to match his cheeky, curious smile, and after three years studying the Genetic Modification of nature and small life forms, he'd climbed the ladder of the corporate genetic giant, Qlipanto.

Jonnie saw what he did at work as kind of a game, and he was good at it; bright, sharp, innovative, and his charismatic demeanour demanded respect, even from those his senior.   But Jonnie didn't really take any of it too seriously, he was in this field really to appease his rich parents – who throughout his youth, pressed, pressured and pushed him to earn the big bucks and to *work hard*.

Jonnie himself would prefer to use his time delving into the depths of Gnosticism, and to be wildly creative; like a horse sprinting bareback through an ocean shoreline. But in his twenties, he was happy to be raking in the bucks, even if it meant his free time suffered.

Jonnie was unorthodox and creative in his work, and after a recent promotion, he could now be even creative.   But the rebel in him was always there, the care free abandon, and the deep desire for something more epic.

It was the autumn of 2017, and Jonnie had just a month ago been placed into a new team with two others. This new small team had a free range to research and experiment at the cutting edge of the companies innovation division; advancing the genetic modification of the vegetable and mineral kingdoms.   They were to be mix, splice, and experiment with as much as they could, including, more secretly, the DNA of insects, small animals, and life forms. This team were seen as a kind of black ops team, and kept away from those who worked mainly with the seeds. This team of three had near unlimited funding and a large amount of slack and free license.

Within the team, Jonnie was the least experienced, and seen as a bit of an up and coming prodigy, and Jonnie was happy to play the junior, and support the other two when they made the big decisions.

Nick in his fifties, and Geoff in his forties, were both very serious, very committed, and pure company men. They both had wrinkles and lines as permanent fixtures in their faces from years of problem solving and serious thinking. Jonnie often thought that if he cut either of them in half it would say Qlipanto all the way through them, like a stick of rock one found at the seaside, but they each bounced off each other professionally, and each had respect for the others. They were a decent team.

Jonnie got a call from one of his Gnostic associates after an all morning meeting. In the meeting Nick, Geoff, and Jonnie were deciding what to do with the three mile square bit of land they'd been given. This land was earmarked to do with whatever they wished - under innovation. There was a loose remit of advancing the companies technical understanding of genetic control within nature, and an unwritten goal of finding something tangible enough to pave the way for some new company owned patents.

Jonnie hadn't heard from Cosa for a while, since the last informal State-Gnostic-meet-up a few months ago. Their friendship went back years to high school days, and oftentimes, *and* infrequently, they both flitted in and out of their friendship that they both knew held longevity.

"Jonnie, you still meddling with mother nature, our mother Sophia?" Cosa quipped in a sarcastic and humorous tone.

"Yeah, well, some of us can't just hang out in Peru all the time drinking strange jungle juice can we?" replied Jonnie.

They both caught up on recent times, plus literature they'd both been reading, and then Cosy came to the crux of the call.

"Jonnie, my new girl and I are hosting a Wachuma ceremony only fifty clicks from your neck of the woods. You know what that is don't you? Or have you been totally assimilated by the mega corporations?"

"Hmm, I remember that being some sort of a psychoactive cactus, heheh, just what've you been up to Cosa?" Jonnie asked with a smile that Cosa could feel and picture in his mind.

"Yes, Elia's been working with it for years, and we decided since we got together, well, we decided to do a little tour of the States - doing healing sessions, you know, only a few people at a time, no more than ten or so. You really have to come Jonnie, you'll love it."

After a slow but meaningful pause, Jonnie replied, "Count me in Cosa," and was as good as there, as Jonnie was always a man of his word.

"Also Jonnie, if you want to bring one or two others, feel free, hey, speak later, and I'll email you some more info and logistics later on. Peace bro."

Jonnie waved his palm, flicking his index finger loosely towards his ear which cut the call, this turned off his TMCD (tattooed mobile communication device), which was a small tattoo behind his ear.

Jonnie sat outside his team's brand new offices, and started to eat his packed lunch (which others in the corporation regularly mocked him about as all the others were in the canteen). He wondered how much Cosa might have changed recently, it was only a year ago he was some years into a successful psychology career, complete with his own practice, but then one trip to Peru had changed all that.

And now he has a Shaman lover, and now he's working with these psychotropic plants, Jonnie thought as he walked back into the office through the silvery-cream arches that were genetically modified vines. The curiousness within him rose, and transmuted to excitement.

*

Jonnie walked to the 'storage and results' laboratory, carrying another mutated rock-stick insect. It was the size of a small soccer ball, at first appearance like a rock, but then one could see its thin legs and joints. It could walk a little clumsily, as if tipsy, but not yet climb or hold balance. Jonnie often messed about with the technology away from any agreed development specifications, and a tiny flower was growing in rock form out of where he could only think its arse should be.

As Jonnie sat it upon the table, and watched it stretch, crawl, walk, and ponder, he too pondered it while it itself pondered. Jonnie's chin was on his crossed arms that lay flat on the table, at eye level with the life form. Jonnie gazed beyond words and labels at what it was, and what it could lead towards, then voices came from the next room…….

"But Nick, she's a nightmare, all she focuses on is how clean everything is or isn't, it's crazy, it's like some DNA strand of OCD (Obsessive Compulsive Disorder) she inherited from her mother just turned itself *on* when we married. If I can get a bit of her DNA I'm sure I can find this OCD gene."

Nick was uncontrollably laughing, but managed to reply to his friend, "Geoff, you've been married for years, you can't be having second thoughts just because she like things to be clean, it's nice she wants things to be clean, you know what us men get like left on our own."

"But Nick, it's not funny anymore – if we're about to have sex she puts a plastic liner down under us as not to dirty the sheets, I can't take it much more." Geoff sighed. "Anyway – how's things at home with you?"

Nick's sniggers morphed to a smile, then to pursed lips, "My issues are different to yours Geoff, my wife's no problem, but it's the son. He's gone into all that anti-system stuff, and keeps going on at me when I watch Fox or CNN news, he goes to those weird festivals with uncooked food and some weird meditations. I'm worried about him…. we're growing distant. He even the other day refused to eat anything that had come from the companies seed industry, he somehow thinks it's unhealthy and unnatural. I think he's on some funny sites using that new eye-implant internet."

Jonnie entered as they continued sharing personal disappointments, stepping his lanky but cool stride, "Hey guys, sorry to overhear, but I know what you guys may both need."

They both looked up and grumbled an "Urrghh" in dazed unison.

Jonnie stood humbly in invitation and put on his best science voice, "A psychologist associate of mine is performing a small gathering soon, with a shaman from Peru. They're using an entheogenic cactus that when drunk can give deep insight into the self and others close to you. Maybe this is what you both need? Well, you're both welcome anyhow."

Geoff and Nick looked at each other in confusion, "Err, thanks Jonnie," frowned Nick, "I'll suppose I'll think about it…. and you Geoff?"

Geoff looked at Jonnie in an open look of desperation at his wife's current characteristics, "I'll do some research and get back to you Jonnie," before he nodded that the matter closed and that work was to being again.

* * *

Jonnie scanned discretely the others in the circle, there were six others including Cosa, Elia, Nick, and Geoff. Elia had long dark wavy hair, dark eyes, and an air of being older than she looked, as if an old wise owl was watching from inside her big brown eyes. Cosa looked younger than he remembered, but more serious and solid, and his energy came less from his head – as if he had surrendered too much thinking to simple awareness. Geoff and Nick looked very out of place, and their casual clothes made them look as awkward as their body language did. The other three consisted of a young couple, and a large tattooed guy who Jonnie vaguely remembered was known locally as having a PCP drug problem.

It was nearly two hours since they'd drunk the large glass of putrid green slime, and the evening shadows lengthened and darkened around the small fire, the fire which Cosa had recently started and nurtured with calm focus.

Their humble gathering was in the middle of a small brush, inbetween the fourteenth and sixteenth holes of a local Golf Course which had closed for the day many hours ago.

Jonnie could feel an uncontrollable nausea, almost claustrophobic, plus a discomfort in his stomach, as if his body was unsure how to accept this medicine, but he caught Elia's knowing look, and the apprehension and excitement increased within him, and in turn, as did the speed of frequency and vibration of his being, as if some figure of eight eternity symbols had came to play and dance inside him, in a soft white and violet haze.

It's getting more wobbly, I can feel the physical realm becoming less hard, less edgy, my toes are starting to buzz and tingle, fingertips too, thought Jonnie, well less like thoughts, more like clear observations.

Jonnie swallowed, and that moved things even more, *ok, that's definitely not normal,* as the taste and energy signature of the cactus infiltrated his being further.

Nausia's passing, wow, I feel expanded, my body is light, as if I'm not in it, or of it, giddy, ok, close eyes......what'll that do.

Images came, some fast, some slow, each with large waves of feeling and energy, colours, fractals, immense geometry, energies alien to him, energies all too familiar, vibrant colours and motion.

Memories came, as if they were all from the now, other images, maybe from future, time became bendy and nonsensical, and Jonnie felt he could float into any of his collected and experienced memories or emotions, and feel it in its entirety, and see the lessons, stories, and causal reasons.

Some of the reasons for such experiences he lived were just so he could feel the emotion, there was no lesson, no solution, it was just to feel the sensation and be with that sensation, as *that* was his karma. He could feel the pain of others where he'd conflicted it, as if he were them, and also feel the joy where he had created it, and see and feel these emotions from any angle of recipient perception.

Minutes or hours passed, he knew not.

Ok, I can definitely feel it....need to pee, must pee before it really takes hold.

Elia knew and looked at him in a way that offered help, but Jonnie, a bit like a slow motion drunk, nodded a polite decline to her. Jonnie walked twenty or so paces from the group, with each step taking his full concentration. As he pee'd he could feel old thought patterns and negativity wash out of him – as if he was purging through his pee – he held the flow, scraped around inside his emotions and thoughts, and mustered a ball of negative energy which was grey and oily – then unleashed it out in his pee in a controlled but strong gush, all on a long out breath. Knowing this may take a while, Jonnie looked up.

He could see the Town below fading into the night, with most of the street lights lit, each feeling unnaturally bright and unstill, as if the lights were each a felt tip unable to leave the page. The town looked like a scab, he could feel the earth wanting to pluck it off to breath and grow. The largest building belonged to a bank, and Jonnie could feel the aggression for money, and in a split second he whisked in a vision from the clerks, up to the managers, to the hedge fund managers, to the dark forces behind the greed and control.

Woooah, snap out of that one, and Jonnie moved his head to the right, where he could just make out the sixteenth green.   Again he fell into vision and witnessed the pure zen focus of mind required to play golf at a high level, and the pure energy of learning a skill. He then again felt the dark forces from investment corporations that sponsor golf, and pulled away from the vision.

The long pee was finished, and a deep breath looking at Venus in the sky brought in light and a new elevated vibration. A feeling of universal connection, of love, of supreme expansion.   Jonnie walked slowly to rejoin the group, moving the body felt to Jonnie like a first time pilot in a large silly costume; fun, exciting, awkward, and a little mischievous.

Don't look at the others, too much information about them comes, as If all our auras are blasted open and ten miles wide. Go inside, lie down, close eyes, go inside, accept her, let it take me further, let her show me, thought Jonnie.

It got stronger, quicker, stronger, like something was softly coaxing him away to another world.

Stories were killed, emotions were purified, the personality was judged, destructed, and putrefied. The self was no-thing, just awareness watching and learning, feeling light, embracing love and harmony in resonant and symbolic forms, feeling darkness and shadow. The inner worlds were infinite, eternal, massive, enormous. Just one thought, word, or image would open up whole dimensions of intelligence and knowledge.

Too intense, see the ....fire, open ...the ....eyes, need to ...feel the group .....to know I can .....get back to ....the body......Nick and Geoff look so dark, so twisted, no, oh no....they look evil, nooooooooooo.

The inner worlds of Gaia pulled Jonnie away to a neon fauna filled garden, and as he walked, the garden slowly became black and tortured, with chemicals, mutated DNA, and toxins all taking over with haste and menace. Then orc-like demons around four foot high came racing in and placed Geoff, Nick, and Jonnie on large crosses to bleed. Smaller dark critters with red eyes jumped from the snarling demons to munch upon on the auras of the three men. The concrete and buildings faded, and then the demons started to mutate any nature that was left, all the while Gaia's pain darted right into the solar plexus of Jonnie and the two others, in a desperate fading violet light, surrounded with growing and glowing red and black streaks.

Jonnie could feel it; the genetic modification of seeds and nature was killing Gaia in *this* garden, and in turn invoking more demons. The hosts of demons then calmed and started to worship the three of them; The Godlike creator-masters of genetic modification, the Demon Kings. As soon as Jonnie had this realisation he aroused more terror and fear in himself, then a thousand more demons came into the arid land, manipulating trees, and mutating flowers into dark fractals that sent darts into the third eyes of other demons – which in turn they laughed and yelled in a warriors victory or cries of joy at their own pain and the chaos around them.

It *was* chaos, supremely unbalanced, and Jonnie and the others had helped create this inner world over years of thought forms and focused energy from their work.

I can't take the pain anymore, I will do anything, I'm so sorry, Jonnie cried inside, and looked over to Nick who looked dead on his cross, and Geoff, who had one eyeball left, and critters eating his maimed feet with pure demonic worship and adoration for their Demon Kings of Chaos.

Jonnie remembered a Gnostic prayer, one of Sophia, the feminine, Gaia, Isis, nature.   He said it with all his being, as if his fingers were slowly losing grip from a cliff face into an abyss that delved into deep hell.

I will cry out with Faith-Wisdom in my heart,
She calls out to the True Light as my soul –
Before the First Mystery I confess,
In my confusion I went to a false light,
And became bound up in shades and shadows,
My light-power being stolen from me,
Because of my misdirected desire!
Looking outward and downward, I have fallen out,
I have come into the darkness of matter and chaos,
And given way to the worship of the demiurge and archons,
Establishing lesser divinities in the place of the First
Commandment –
On account of the illusion of separation, the delusion of lack,
I did not did not go within and live within to cleave,

But apart from my Beloved I have created,
And what I have created is my bondage!
O Sophia, I call upon your name,
Grant me clemency in the darkness of matter and chaos,
I repent of darkness of ignorance I have engendered,
O True Light, have mercy upon me and deliver me,
Send forth your Pure Emanation,
Restore my light-power to me!
Amen.

All of a sudden a burst of white light blew away the whole scene in the garden. Demons exploded, imploded, and faded – all in yells of desire to be close to their kings that fed them. Then layers of green faded in - pink, light green, softness, like a morning mist clearing for beauty. Birds sang, swooped, and danced. Trees, plants, and wondrous flowers popped up sending tiny child-like fairies into the air to dance. It was like popcorn of divinity filling the space.

Tiny elves and fairies were slightly seen and felt; running, whisping, hiding, laughing. Never a clear look upon one, but fleeting glances and trails of their energy. The energy of love became strong – like smooth waves of healing upon the three of them, who now sat knelt on the daisy strewn fresh grass in humility and shame.

She floated in with the sun's rays behind her, a goddess, an angel, an elf princess – the labels were unable to be grasped - but she came – shimmering, without edges, without judgement – she stood before them – pure, forgiving, caring, nurturing.

She stood before them in pure humility and grace as the elementals followed close to her and danced in her aura. She bowed her soft face of care, and spoke with a tone like silk cutting through a lake. "Boys, redeem yourself with your land you have –

you know what to do with this vision I will show you.   Send a message to those that invoke demons upon Gaia by mutilation of her soul.   Share vision, share love, care for your mother that gives, and redemption is yours."

Then the groups of small elemental beings from the elf, gnome, and fairy worlds sprawled out from behind her, and danced upon the rays of the sun, they continued their dance in flight into each of their three auras.   They shared a vision, from where they knew not, but the vision was clear, loving, and beautiful.

BAM.

The fire crackled, Elia looked at Jonnie with loving eyes, as if she'd been witness to much of what happened. Geoff and Nick were being sick through their bodies that appeared only just alive – as if the only life in them were the stomachs releasing pain through the fluid in their mouths.   Geoff and Nick caught a glimpse of each other, and some humour climbed up and began to reign, they started to try to laugh through battered eyes, through the tears, through the dribbling. They were alive, they would be redeemed.

Jonnie lay for the next hour in pure gratitude for his being, for his vessel, for the refreshed position he was in. He knew what to do, and knew Geoff and Nick also knew too. After another hour of laying and experiencing this newness, this rebirth, this soft return to the gift of human life on earth, Jonnie looked around.

The young couple were staring deeply into each other with love, the PCP guy looked like an innocent child in bliss, Cosy and Elia were still holding the space etherically, and Geoff and Nick each had less than half the wrinkles and frown lines they had before the night began. Cosa looked over to Jonnie, and winked with a smile, Jonnie giggled back with a smile that was pure gratitude born from other worlds.

**

Two months later, Jonnie, Geoff, and Nick waited at the edge of
the piece of land they'd been given to work with, ready with a
complimentary drinks and canapés reception.   The sun had
already risen and the oranges in the sky were giving way to lighter
blues.

The Chief Executive and the two major shareholders from the
Qlipanto Board of Directors arrived in separate but identical black
Mercedes,' each with a tiny Qlipanto flag attached to the logo at
the front of the shiny bonnets.

The three walked from their cars and slowly converged together in
a speechless march. They had not even glanced at each other due
to the sight before them. Their mouths opened and eyes
widened, each eager to take in the all of the wonder of what they
were witnessing.

Before the six humans stood a Gaia Utopia.   A large town that was
formed and functioning solely from life in the mineral and
vegetable kingdoms.

Large leaves were empty magic carpets whisping around the air
elegantly, each awaiting humans. Trees and vines grew together,
moulding and merging into tree based housing complexes.
Branches and wood moved within the live structures to allow for
moving steps and platforms. Pod beds appeared below branches,
appearing like a type of cotton and wool insulation that could
grow and morph.   Grass vine homes could be seen, growing and
shrinking, morphing, so one could see the different design
potentials.

Water ran through stone runs and through stone mills, channels of
water ran through the inside of hollow gateway trees, redirecting
water to different areas through long tubular branches, bamboo,
and vines.

High crop trees existed, with different fruit and vegetables growing on different levels, some looked planted, but some looked a part of this mega-food-tree itself.

Pyramid and dome houses out of straw, cob, and soil all linked together with corridors, and all the light and electricity was supplied by a type of smiling firefly. In one area, groups of fireflies in pods were eating hemp and maca, and somehow turning this into larger quantities of electricity.

In another area, trees grew firewood as fruit; twigs, small branches and logs each grew and fell off in moments. One lit itself, and gave heat straight away, and after some minutes none of the wood seemed to have died.

The sun, wind, and rain were all used in relationships with the living town. Human waste all had relationships with the living metropolis too.

Spaces of manifest existed too, where humans could experiment further with the intelligence of the town, where also children could create play areas out of earth and grass with their imaginations.

If it rained large lilies with wings from a wasp would swoop down to be used as umbrellas, and some other vegetation was producing clothes.

In all of this, each shape was natural and harmonic, with subtle sways of geometry weaving through the space, ready for human beings to harness and use.

"H…..Ho…..just how did you three do it? Show us the DNA codes at once, show us the manipulation of nature! Does anyone else know about this?" Stuttered the Chief Executive in frothing excitement and authority, but also in a state of jaw dropping, surreal, disbelief.

"We had help that you wouldn't believe," Jonnie retorted, "The why's and how's are complex."

"Other help? Contractors? It was just meant to be just you three! But we can discuss the details later. Tell me more about this place, what would people who live in these towns do?" Marched the Chief Executive.

Geoff spoke through his thin smile, "Create, innovate, live, study themselves, gain knowledge, and evolve."

"Ok, I can see it, I think we can market this, It's going to be worth billions and billions!" One of the Directors chirped up, and the three bosses united their energy in greedy glee.

Jonnie then waved his hand, and it all stopped. The leaves and vines all fell to the floor, the wood that was moving In scores of different ways all creaked to a standstill. Water started to overflow in places, stop in others, and flow into areas it wasn't supposed to.   Manipulated trees dropped their fruits in a sigh of relief. It looked broke, off, dormant, as if a jungle had been starved of daylight for a week.

"Whaaat are you doing, is this some sort of joke? Turn it all back on immediately, and give me the design paperwork," stormed the chief executive.

Jonnie squared to the three bosses and spoke, "Humanity's not ready for this yet, our species can do this naturally, but we're not ready.   The three of us quit as of now. We know that what we've been doing is wrong, and with the information we have, we're going share our knowledge online about the ills of Qlipanto. It's not right, we need to evolve consciousness and evolve past greed and anger before this is even thought about."

The three executives looked at each other, "Urrghh?"

Cosa and Elia were camping in a nearby wood. They giggled as they knew what Jonnie and his team were up to.   They sang a poem as they packed up their items ready to move on up state for another ceremony;

And the Great Mother said:
Come my child and give me all that you are.
I am not afraid of your strength and darkness, of your fear and pain.
Give me your tears. They will be my rushing rivers and roaring oceans.
Give me your rage. It will erupt into my molten volcanoes and rolling thunder.
Give me your tired spirit. I will lay it to rest in my soft meadows.
Give me your hopes and dreams. I will plant a field of sunflowers and arch rainbows in the sky.
You are not too much for me. My arms and heart welcome your true fullness.
There is room in my world for all of you, all that you are.
I will cradle you in the boughs of my ancient redwoods and the valleys of my gentle rolling hills.
My soft winds will sing you lullabies and soothe your burdened heart.
Release your deep pain. You are not alone and you have never been alone.
-Linda Reuther

Then, together they prayed for the land;

Father, when You created the first couple, You put them in an exquisite garden so they could steward it wisely. You knew that in the act of caring for creation, they would also find abundance of provision. I confess that mankind in general has abandoned caring for the land under the excuse of needing to extract resources from

the land, and this exploitation is sin. I ask You to open the books
from the day the first human walked on this land, to the present,
and to cleanse the land from every sin of overt exploitation as well
as the more rampant sin of neglect. Forgive humanity for not
walking in stewardship on this land. It is a masterpiece, crafted by
Your hands, and mankind has too often shown contempt for You,
the Master Craftsman, by treating the land as a personal
possession to be used and exploited.

A Dark Honour

In 2017 the world was in more of a mess; food was in shorter supply, oil and gas prices had rocketed, corruption and lies within corporations, governments, and media had gotten worse, Internet users were DNA surveyed, the middle east was a battleground for military muscle, the Stock Market ran on a manipulative AI, the weather was voilent, and Google was soon to launch driverless cars in thirty cities, after the success of their new tattooed ear-chip.

Coinciding with this was many cities desperate riots due to poverty and hunger, and many people went the other way, living far away from the metropolis' in nature - foraging and going back to basics.

In this time there were a cloaked band of around two hundred people from all over the world called 'Honour.' They were tirelessly making documentaries, supporting hacker groups that took big corporate sites down (temporarily), and getting messages out via art and music. All the time using social online media with fake internet passports.

But the net was closing in, eighteen of them were tracked down and arrested in a heavy handed joint effort between the CIA and the NSA, in which the two members of 'Honour' had been shot dead in a stand-off. 'Honour' had been targeted more heavily since their increase in direct action, most notably the hacking into every compulsory iPad that western schools gave their pupils. The hacking itself presented a five minute video showing the ills of the world elite and the knock on affect on the earth. It showed how the education system created tax-paying worker drones with little creativity. Schools weren't the same since what had become known as *The Honour-iHack*; Riots, non-attendance, and graffiti now reigned in most schools, and this movement was spreading like wildfire. The five minute clip became the most viewed movie in the history of the planet.

In the stormed siege to arrest Honour, one young man was brutally shot dead for not raising his hands as he ran, then another youth who must have been a close friend of the other, walked slowly and purposefully into the ring of the armed SWAT team as he repeated, "Shoot me too" with his hands in his pockets. They shot him dead. But this event was filmed and uploaded by some of the others in the old derelict building before they were arrested, and it went viral.

This really pissed off the elite and media, who before the iHack incident all saw 'Honour' as a kind of fun nemesis, something they could play with and demonise. But now all efforts were now fixed onto finding the remaining two hundred or so 'terrorists,' as they were now labelled.

The game was nearly up for Honour.

In an encrypted server cluster with IP's changing every few seconds, most of Honour's members met up in an online IRC chat to decide what to do. They had no leader or hierarchy but each had a skill or gift to add to the pot, and in their rare meetings like this, someone was randomly asked to chair and hold the agenda and flow of proceedings.

The meeting lasted three hours, and each member agreed to the plan and its secrecy.

*

The next day the plan went into action, and lasted fourteen days. Each action was streamed live online, then spread on social sites and the blogosphere within minutes. Each went mega viral and the CIA and NSA just couldn't stop it.

Five people jumped from an offshore BP oil rig near Libya with full barrels of oil tied to their feet. Each fell to the bottom of the ocean to drown.

Two people dressed in Military fatigues ran frantically into the USA drone Headquarters in Colorado with old sound cards attached to their chests, both were shot.

Twenty people ran into HSBC headquarters in London and stuffed fifty pound notes laced with anthrax into their mouths, each died in seconds.

Six people ran into a busy McDonalds in Sydney, and stuffed Big Macs laced with poison into their mouths. Each died in minutes.

Three people went to Monsanto's experimental fields in Southern Spain and nailed themselves to crosses. It was remote. Each died over the course of three days.

One person went to Fleet Street with each of the days' Newspapers glued to him. He tipped petrol on himself, and lit a match.

Four others in the Pacific dressed themselves as sardines and tuna and covered their outfits with the respective meat. They then waited on a small raft three miles out from a small island near Tahiti. Each were maimed to death by sharks.

Ten people went to the Amazon and climbed a massive tree. Each jumped off head first.

One person broke into the BBC evening newsroom with a TV on his head, in a way so that his face was were the screen would be. He burst into where the newsreader was reading his script, and the TV imploded, like a reverse explosion –crushing his head to a pulp and sending blood everywhere.

Five people went into Wallmart in Dallas, and once at the till to pay for a trolley full of their most toxic and unethical products, each fell to his death, presumed to be from a high-tech, timed-based poison.

Four people went into a cancer chemotherapy unit in Tokyo, and after leaving raw fruit and veg everywhere, they dropped like flies, again, thought to be using the poison.

Three people broke into Smithkline Beechams and swallowed scores of tablets from the profit making production line. Each died two days later.

Five people broke into a Google driverless car, and programmed it to drive off Beachy Head cliffs in England.

This went on for days, and the whole world was watching. Each dead body had the Tattoo – "Sacrificial-Honour."

Nothing could seem to stop the Sacrificial-Honour, it was daily and nobody knew where, when, or how. Honour were so advanced online that they always seemed to outwit the NSA, intelligence agencies, and media.

Then after near two hundred had given their lives, a video appeared on the internet as a live stream.

"Hi, I'm Jake. The last member of Honour. We are truly sorry for any pain we have caused, but you all know deep down, this pain is nothing compared to what the earth has suffered, or what our children's children will suffer if something's not done. We had nothing to lose, we were all about to spend the rest of our lives in prisons.

You know our motto, *To objectively leave a better planet for the next generation holds the highest honour.* There is honour in dying for what you believe in, there always has been and always will be. Here is just a ride, and for some of us, the toxicity was so powerful we were happy and blissful to die for this cause. We leave you, Honour."

Jake appeared calm, focused, and very zen, almost as though he'd spent most of his life in meditation and in nature.   He then drank a large glass of Ayahausca, about a pint, and for the next four hours the world just watched…………he was not coming back. It was as if he took on the pain of all of his brothers who'd died, then the pain of the planet, then that of all of humanity through millennia, then one racing and powerful bright spark brightened his eyes – it could only be described as pure wonder, then he left this realm.   The body sat limp but seemed to still radiate a heat, a warmth - something universal was still close to the body but Jake had a while a go left the physical realm.

*

Jake inspired something into the youth of the world, most of whom were hungry for a true role model, devoid of opportunity, oppressed, or living in a debt bubble that was not even their creation. By the following week, over a thousand more Sacrificial-Honours had occurred worldwide.   A new mega-meme had exploded, and was exponentially gaining momentum.

Some became more extreme; entertainment venues, celebrity parties, corporate stores selling toxins in food, and offices of system authority were all targeted.   Each time never a bomb or firearm was used, nobody else was hurt, and more and more creative ways were presented.   Most importantly for them as it was held as their trademark, each Sacrificial-Honour was streamed to the internet.

People still living within the mental psyche of the old system became scared, nowhere for them was safe, they had nowhere to look but within themselves……..and slowly, very slowly, but very surely, things began to change.

Ascenders 22

Janco was mildly anti-social, mainly due to some of the principles he lived by. He cared for the animals and the planet for as long as he could remember, he could *feel* their pain, and also etherically *see* their pain. He'd spent many years working directly with a variety of animals and trees, and had also spent time and energy in various forms of activism. But at twenty nine years of age, he'd stopped working so much at the symptoms, and had been studying more the root causes of the suffering - corporate policies, and ultimately their greed, plus the lies and conditioning from the main stream media.

Being 2014, and being without much care for the latest gadgets or fashion, Janco was labelled a greeny or a hippy by many. He cared little as he knew both were media created labels for people who cared for life, but who got in the way of the status-quo.

Recently on some web-based alternative news channels, Janco had seen separate tales of some amazing stories of strange children performing amazing healings. The children just more or less appeared amongst strangers, healed with their hands, then left. The main stream news had a blackout on this, but the alternative sites and social media were starting to spin up into debate and theory.

After a few months, near half of the western population knew something about these amazing stories of unexplainable child healings. No face recognition or identity of the children was gained for some irrational reason, and they never spoke. Oftentimes it seemed impossible for the children to have reached their location, and in some recent CCTV footage, which was the best footage gained since the stories started, it was is if they had the presence to quieten others, to soften the space, and to pacify surrounding humans.

The stories and reports increased.

Janco was at his allotment where he often went to find peace from life in the London suburbs. Here he grew enough vegetables to make a living by selling organic boxes to the middle and upper classes in west London.

The thick sheet of grey cloud above darkened, and spits of water started to fall. Janco wiped the sweat from his dark brow and entered his little crooked shed to take shelter. As Janco munched on a funny shaped carrot (that he knew the Chelsea types wouldn't approve of in their organic boxes), tools and seed trays on the shelf started to shake, then flashing light filled both of the small square windows. The light got brighter and the flashes more frequent. *Whaaat, am I hallucinating?* thought Janco, as he looked at his carrot to see if there was any strange chemicals on it, possibly blown from the allotment three across from his.

"Hi Janco," said a small boy standing in front of him. The boy looked about seven, blonde hair, and pure faced, with piercing bright eyes that immediately showed he was carrying wisdom far beyond his years.

"May I?" the boy asked, as he grabbed a parsnip and started to munch upon it before Janco could answer. Janco was frozen in shock, the boy hadn't come through the door, he would've heard it, even through the rhythmic noise of the rain on the corrugated metal roof.

"Janco, do you know who and what I am, and why I'm here?" The boy asked as he played calmly with some of the tools, as a typical seven year old would.

"You….you……are you one of them? One of the child healers?" Janco was getting nervous. "This can't be happening, I'm not ill or unwell, I live a simple life, what would you want with me?" Janco was near shaking in fright, excitement, and bewilderment, and gripped his carrot more fiercely as his palms pored fresh sweat.

"Calm down Janco, hehe, I'm only seven, Shai's the name. There's nothing to fear."

Shai moved to stand in front of Janco, but looking around for things to play with.

"I came to you *because* you live a simple life, you have a good heart, and I've had a change in my Ascenders 22 deliberations."

"You're going to have to back up little one, how am I to know of what you've deliberated? And don't jump on that crate Shai, I need that…ffff!"

"Oops, sorry. Ah, of course, you don't know, heheh " Shai said as he skipped from the crate towards the new toy of a spade handle.

"Ok, seven of us souls behind the veil made a pact. To come back to earth to help." Shai looked more deeply at Janco, "We each evolved out of the cycle of death and rebirth here, but we chose to come back, to give something back to a reality construct that gave *us* so much."   Shai slowed his play and started to look more wise, as if his soul was alive with remembrance from scores of past lives.

"Janco, we can heal, we can move through walls, we can manifest, soften energy, go into people's dreams, be highly empathic, and travel at speed. We can see virtues and vices as if they were cars or boats, and we can remove astral parasites from a person or place."

Janco knew this to be true, it was as if his intuition and soul were being vibrated with a poignant experience, one of those life changing moments where everything slowed down and sped up.

"B...but what about your parents Shai? Do others *know* of you, who you are, what you do?" Janco said as he remained what seemed glued to his chair.

Shai placed his child exuberance aside, "We came here in these seven year old forms exactly a year ago today. We didn't seek to have parents as it would've caused too many ripples, too much pain or confusion for other souls."

Janco nodded for Shai to continue. "We also didn't desire re-doing the baby thing, being stuck in box rooms with animal toys that looked nothing like the real animals, or going through the conditioning of school where one is taught that Apple, Ball, and Cat are the most important things for a human to know first." Shai walked slowly around the tiny area in front of Janco as the rain pelted the roof.

"You see Janco, each spring equinox, which is today you may or not know, the seven of us can each choose 22 more humans to be part of us, to see what we can see, to share in our abilities, and today Mister Janco, I'm choosing you!"

Janco had never really been into healing, spirituality or religion, but he always knew and felt something else existed. He also believed in reincarnation and the power of the mind, and knew stillness, but never really gave these subjects or concepts any more thought than that.

"No way little one, not me, I don't want it, and nor do I need it. I'm quite happy with my life, and I'm no healer or saviour, nor do I seek to be. I see pain in this reality, also falsehood and idiocy, I'm the last person you should choose." Janco said in his most adamant tone, as he glanced at the leak coming in through the top corner of the shed from the now hammering rain, almost in a show that he had more important mundane things to deal with.

"Janco, rejoice that you see these things, for it's your Salvation that draweth nigh, and not your Doom." Shai looked more seriously at Janco, "Beyond the forged identity and physical domain there are places of unimaginable majesty, and nature of unspeakable depth and beauty. You can only see splinters of that eternal domain in the physical here." Shai started to turn slowly in small circles, almost on a six pence, "However Janco, when you humans here ever set the fear and hostility aside, the world of eternity unmasks itself and presents itself even to your physical senses-"

 "-I'm still not interested Shai. I'll see all that when I die. What are you? Some sort of ascension salesman?"

Shai ignored the comment with a wry grin and continued.

"Janco, society is like a stew. If it isn't stirred up every once in a while, the good stuff sinks to the bottom and a layer of scum floats to the top. This is what's happened on Earth, and you know it. You've no boss, or close family, you create so few ripples, so unfortunately you have no say, I'm choosing you, and I really hope you take it well."

"There's nothing noble in being superior to another man Shai! Surely true nobility is in being superior to ones previous self. So please leave me alone!"

Shai remained within a pure calm of knowingness.

"Janco, you know the issues, the world doesn't need more successful people. It needs more poets and writers and dreamers. It needs more people who are *awake*. It needs more kindness and cooperation. It needs spirits who are willing to tell the truth, and sink to their knees in supplication. Man's a fallen god who doesn't really belong in this world Janco. Mans original fatherland is the Other World, which doesn't belong to the visible. The human being with his microcosmic light-spark wanders through the world of good and evil and is constantly tormented by its opposites........"

Janco wiped his brow and tried to block Shai's words and resonance, but he could feel their vibration inside him. Is *this a trick?* Janco thought.

Shai continued, ".....But this balance of good and evil has been hacked, evil reigns and is ravenously hungry. You are chosen for you've a courageous heart. I've made my decision Janco, and have another fourteen people to go and see before the sun sets tonight." Shai moved forward and touched Jancos hand. "I now liberate you from the delusion that this transient world is the true world. I wish you well."

Light filled the room and the shelves and tools began to shake. Shai had now disappeared.

*

Janco stumbled out the shed, feeling super self aware, and also trying and feel any difference. *Hmmm, not much seems different, wait a minute.* The vegetables growing in his allotment sent the energy of life to him, of intelligence, of the desire to live, the desire for light, the desire for water, the desire for nurture, and the playful desire to multiply and survive. He looked across at the allotment three across and could see and feel the pain of the vegetables, covered in chemical pesticides, crying out for help in their mutated and inorganic states. He felt a deep sadness as the pain reached inside his soul, and then Janco knew he had to get out of there, to get home and let things settle, to go were less life was!

As Janco thought of his front room at home, he saw wavy violet light strands come up from below him, and then in just three seconds all the paths and roads that took him home flashed before him in perfect order. Janco then found himself in his front room as the wavy violet light strands fell down into the floor around him. *Ok, that must be the fast travel Shai mentioned,* Janco thought to himself nervously, as he noticed he'd just gone through two doors without opening them. Janco gulped as he sat down to calm the shaking, and soon fell into a fourteen hour dreamless sleep, as his vessel and being took in the changes.

*

Janco awoke and knew straight away the changes. He could feel them instantly. He still felt the same in his mind and thought streams, but he was energetically wider, taller, more expansive, and could feel more. *But what to do?* *Where to go?* Janco contemplated in confusion for over an hour before he made some breakfast and turned the TV on. Before he could grab the remote control he felt the darkness of a female celebrity singer being interviewed. She was one that was often on MTV acting like a whore, and Janco could feel her soul in pain. Her soul was almost completely lost as it was given away and sold to others to appease her greedy desire for fame.

Janco thought of her and felt for her location. Fzzzzz, the violet streaks flowed upwards, and he was off. Door, road, up, houses, roads, shoreline, sea, sea, more sea, New York, theatre, upstairs, penthouse, all in five seconds. The violet streaks of light spiralled down into the floor.

Only Millie and Janco were in the room, and Millie was clearing off her make up in front of a mirror. Alongside her was a half finished (long) line of coke, and a half drunk champagne bottle. She froze, but quickly calmed as she noticed Janco in the mirror, as if her soul overrode her egoistic mind, and *let* Janco in. Millie swivelled in the chair to face him, and Janco willed her to bow her head. Janco could see the vice of giving one's body away sexually for fame, as though it was a solid object.   Quickly Janco's vision changed, and he saw her as just pure energy. He dipped his hands into her geometric codes to push source love energy into her being.   After thirty or so seconds it was as if a large eel was becoming visible and starting to panic for survival. Janco grabbed it and threw it into the candle to the right of the dressing table. Janco could then see all of her memories, and grabbed the ones of her when she was young with her mum and sister, a time of purity and love. He showed Millie many of the images etherically, and tears started to pour down her face. It was as if her soul had been taken from a dungeon and placed into a field of lavender.

"Millie, grow your soul, the industry you're in is controlled by toxic and evil beings. Do what you Will, but remember this encounter." And with that Janco light-streaked off, back to his front room, and quickly unplugged the TV before falling into a four hour sleep on the sofa.

*

Janco spent the next weeks getting to know his new abilities.   He mainly went to symptoms of problems, such actors playing parts for social engineering, hiphop artists who promoted hustling, and designers of console games that promoted transhumanism and violence. Each time he went in, healed the soul, then left, and never checked up on the aftermath – mainly due to his own internal fear of not doing things right.

Janco knew there must now be one hundred and sixty one of them darting around the planet performing healings, but he blocked himself off from going online to read about them and quashed any desire to contact any of them. Instead, he went to the allotment to find sanity.   Janco in the next few weeks continued to heal, sleep a lot, work the allotment, and take the odd light-streak to some wild and remote landscape where he could contemplate and rebalance.

He knew it was a one-way street, that each step forward on this newfound path irrevocably modified the content of him. It followed that he became more and more of a stranger to his surroundings; that he lost more and more interest in exterior life, in which only a short while ago he participated fully. The appearance of things underwent a deep change in his eyes. He saw that certain faces which only recently he found very beautiful, now revealed to him marks of bestiality behind their features.

One day in late summer Janco had been getting ready at home to visit a reporter for The Sun newspaper (one who reported on female celebrities in London's nightlife), when a circle of violet light-streaks came up from his front room floor, just two metres in front of him.

"Hi Janco" She said. She was tall and slender, with an elegant and unrevealing face, that her dark hair came across in loose strands. "Hope you don't mind me popping in?" She asked.

"Who the hell are you? What do you want?" Janco said, less politely than he intended.

"Chill Janco, I'm Sarien, many of us hang out together and perform group work, mainly on military personnel at the moment." Sarien shugged, "I knew you worked alone from what Shai told me, so I wanted to say hi and see how....hmm, and who you are, oh, and deliver a message."

Janco made Sarein a drink and made an effort to be more welcoming, he never contemplated anyone from the group coming to see him, though it did now make some sense to him and he started to relax.

"So, how are you finding things Sarien? I feel amazing to tell you the truth, but a little alienated and isolated, but I guess this is the price we pay." They chatted for hours sharing stories, ethics, aims, and goals, including Sarien's *change experience*, and her focus on hospital workers, and bullies in different aspects of modern life.

They could both see and feel each other's old vices and small dots in their pasts that remained from painful emotional stories. This created a warm unavoidable honesty and care between them. A closeness.   They did a combined healing on each other, and hugged afterwards within their connection.   Janco had never thought he might need healing as he was healing others.   But he did, he needed to recharge and a regroup within himself, away from the pain of *out-there*.

"Janco, the main reason I came is to tell you there's a meeting for all of us on the autumn equinox. It's somewhere in the Sahara desert so we can keep it private to just the group. Obviously tell no one.....oh, and it's expected we all go for at least the morning, so I super hope to see you there."   Sarien handed Janco the invite.

Janco held it but kept his gaze upon her warm smile, "Sarien, I sometimes think we've been dumped on a hellworld circus, upon the backdrop of natural beauty, all some sort of cosmic joke."

"Janco, dear one, it's not right to groan over the state of the world as if it were lost. What's actually happening is a clash between the old spirit and the new, a clash which is especially noticeable because the old spirit is realising how old it is, and how nothing is looked at any longer from its point of view......" Sarien paused to open a packet of crisps, rolling her eyes at Janco with self annoyance before continuing, "....Try and see it from a broader perspective, and just help where you can. I have to go now, but will see you in the desert, much love." She stroked his face, and then the lights appeared and streaked down around her, and she vapourised in a quiet whisp.

Janco decided to still work alone as he didn't want to get into too many ethical debates – he knew what he knew, knew his abilities, and felt good in that space.

In the coming weeks Janco healed and awoke some twisted souls who were press reporters and news readers, and also visited the quiet introverts sitting alone under trees. He still had a strange internal block on visiting those who damaged the souls of animals and those who damaged the natural world, whether directly or indirectly. He knew he was helping in some way at the moment, and he found enough comfort in this to suppress this strange blockage.

He started to visit members of the Green party, an organisation he once supported years ago. He healed those who gave their souls to two incredible paradox's. The first being that they had no policy against multi-national corporations or central banks, and the second that they supported and played roles in mass centralisation of power by aiming to get more members into the EU parliament. But on these visits he realised the people were using their time and energy within the party to appease and suppress personal issues, using the party as a gasket to release energy and build etheric walls and shields.

*

Western Society (especially within the Internet) was going into fever over these empathic visitors, these healers. Though there was still a main stream media blackout, most people in the western world now chatted about it at least once or twice a week.

The circus had begun.

Cults were formed that worshipped the healers. Detective-like research groups hunted them and their past, and now five of the group had now been exposed with their past scattered over the alternative news sites. Fakers and charlatans were growing, each pretending to be one of the group, or that they were aquatinted with them. New-age channellers claimed to channel the group or the aliens that controlled them, or the aliens that were within them. Other conspiracy groups attacked them, mainly stating they were either a CIA created project or a mind control experiment, and spiritual groups and main stream religions praised them or attacked them for affecting their notions of karma and humility.

But in the big picture, people *were* healing, people *were* waking up, anything from twenty to a hundred souls a day, and those newly awakened knew hundreds of other people, so the ripples where slowly spreading around the lake of life on earth.

But ultimately and relatively, in the corporate, political, and military arenas, not too many were visited by the healers.   The powers that be just replaced any recently awakened (who always resigned or quit) with one from the queues of other psychopaths looking for *work* in these sectors.

The roots of society still held firm whilst the branches were starting to shake in the new winds.

*

Janco light-streaked to the desert, re-materialising over a kilometre away from where the meeting would soon start. Here he could find some solace and peace before the massive wafts of energy from the meeting would pierce into his perception.

Soon Janco started to walk slowly over the dunes, stopping at the top of each to take in the views and serenity.   Over another dune and there it was, a large sweeping white marquee with a small stage, with a Moroccan style decor for the group members to relax in. *Very nice, I wonder how they set all this up?* Thought Janco as he now began to pass other people who lived a similar existence to himself. *It's as if a secret race of around a hundred were having a secret party.*

Respect, smiles, and nods were shared, as any formality to the space soon dropped into a mutual care and respect.

A small boy with dark hair strolled the stage to the centre, and parted his arms humbly, "Thank you all so much for coming, thank you so, so much, Now please, get yourselves comfortable, and feel free to take any nibbles and drinks with you. We'll start very soon."

As Janco grabbed a plate of twiglets, he saw Sarien pouring two drinks. She turned with finesse, "One for you Janco, one for me, shall we sit?" Janco knew she had used her empathic abilities to locate him, as he was about to too. They smiled at each other in the shared knowledge.

It was not as if any of the group turned their abilities on or off though, it was as more a whole and normal part of them. And this was the case with Sarien for sure.

A hush fell over the informal seating areas as seven children, four boys and three girls, entered the stage to take their seats. Looking objectively a bit like an informal conference about toys or sweets.

Next to Shai sat the boy with the dark hair who spoke shortly before, sitting in the middle of three others either side. He stood up and started to stroll, no microphone was required as the abilities of the children could telepathically beam the words telepathically at different sensitivities for different people.

"Welcome all, I'm known as Beaquo. We thought to get us all together as what, six months have passed, and to re-group and share." Beaquo was a little taller than the other children, and strolled with confidence, as though coming back to earth and helping the planet was just a little morning chore. "We were hoping all one hundred and sixty one would be here, but alas, eleven are not present. So let us start with this news to stop any gossip. Three left this reality of their own choice, suicide in earth terms. They wanted to taste more from behind the veil. We don't recommend this as one will be reborn into a denser reality. We probably should've explained this around the time of the changes, an oversight on our part. Apologies"   Janco joked internally a while back that some sort of welcome pack would have helped and looked to Sarien to share his inner humour. Sarien returned a friendly scowl.

Beaquo continued, "Another two lost their vessels in travel accidents. One ended up in the middle of a large rock, and another crashed into a large plane. Be careful out there." Some murmurs from the seated crowd came and went before Beaquo continued, "….Another three have not turned up, and are officially AWOL, is that right Shai?"

Shai nodded before he himself spoke, "Yes, three have been missing for four months, but we know they are on earth somewhere. The fear with this is that we chose poorly with one or two, and they fell into self-cherishing narcissism Beaquo."

"Thanks Shai….."

To Janco listening, it was as though a salesman had just chipped in some technical information.

"…..Three others have been murdered, one by a tribe in deep Africa, one by the CIA, and one by MOSSAD.   So later if you wish to give your respects to those deceased, then there is a shrine out back with photos and flowers."   There was a silent respectful pause, before Beaquo presented another of the seven, "So thank y'all for coming, and now Louisa will talk for a while."

Beaquo sat, and the cute looking Louisa took to the cente of the stage. Her feminine smile took precedence over her pony tailed light hair, and she gave off a feeling as though she was part of the earth herself.

Louisa spoke for twenty minutes, with Janco and Sarien feeling supreme warmth in the last comment she made, "The absorbing interest of the present day is that the world is growing itself a new skin. We realise that the heavy mantle of the past, of all those things which no longer have any meaning for our minds, is slipping irrevocably away and leaving our souls free...." The crowd were falling into her words as she continued, "....The horizon broadens and lights up instead of closing down upon itself and becoming more and more obscure. I want this to be your attitude. I find that it brings peace and serenity to all those whom I am able to persuade of its truth."

It was obvious to all there that no leader existed within the seven children who'd come back to help humanity. It was almost like one soul had split into seven so it could be at many places and do many things at the same time.

Shai spoke too for a while, "In every age there's been scattered forerunners in the world. They're those who are ahead of their time, and whose personal action is based on an inward knowledge of that which is yet to come. If you and I should happen to be forerunners, let us bless it, even though, living a century or two too soon, we may feel ourselves to be strangers in a foreign land........" Janco could feel that most of the group could relate to Shai's words, ".....Because others cannot vibrate in your experience, they cannot affect the outcome of your experience. They can hold their opinions, but unless their opinion affects your opinion, their opinion matters not. A million people could be pushing against you, and it wouldn't negatively affect you unless you push back. They're affecting what happens in *their* experience. They're affecting *their* point of attraction. So set aside everything which might make you at all touchy or timid and let all your qualities of goodwill, frankness and simplicity shine forth in your dealings with everyone you meet. Never mind how different their characters and way of life may be."

The bald boy on the end was next to speak, "Hi everyone, there's one overriding reason we've asked you to come here. You surely all remember on the vernal equinox back in March, each of us seven here chose twenty-two of you to experience our sensitivity and abilities, to be part of our healing and evolution on earth. Well, we're giving you each another gift. On the coming Vernal Equinox, just six months from now, you can each choose one other to join this group we're a part of, to share in our sight, empathy, healing, and abilities. You will have from sunrise until sunset on the Equinox in any part of the world to make your choice. Ponder it well, and chose wisely!"

Murmurs quickly rose into a din of talking, covered with the etheric signatures of bewilderment, responsibility, and excitement.

Once things calmed, a girl known as Erin stood up and spoke, "Rejoice in the light which you've been given, and don't be surprised that it's so difficult to pass it on to others. It really is making its way, not so much through you or me as through force of circumstance. You are simply ahead of your time." Erin seemed very angelic, and far from the dense mundane world, but she packed into a small and elegant vessel. "Intelligent people can no longer deceive themselves about old systems and old ideas. Circumstances having radically changed and changed beyond possibility of recall. Such people are in just the same situations you were. It's a situation which often seems hard but is in reality infinitely less hard than the contrary situation would be. For that would mean living in falsehood and driving into falsehood new generations who would be bound to suffer." Erin received the most rousing reception from the crowd of the morning.

More short protocol and health and safety talks went on for thirty minutes or so, followed by a short question and answer session that gave Janco little more than he already knew.

The session moved into an informal lunchtime; meet and greet / mingle session, and Janco was done, it was not his thing. He quietly left making sure he left little etheric signature in his exit. He also wanted to slope off before the afternoon sessions, where once in small groups they would brainstorm challenges the world faced regarding its evolution trajectories. Janco felt he knew enough and didn't want his knowledge or direction diluted, polluted, or questioned.

Three minutes later Janco sat under a palm tree next to a beautiful Oasis.

From nowhere, Sarien light-streaked up from the shore of the water, "Voila, hi Janco, I brought us some lunch before I sneaked out," and smilingly nudged him over in a friendly way to share the shade. Sarien could feel where he was as Janco had his etheric wall lowered to her, almost like a constant invite. But if others in the marquee wondered where they were, they wouldn't be able to know, save the seven children of course.

"Janco, why did you leave? There's still things you can learn there today"

"I know, it's just I'm not looking to heal people in pain so much, I'm looking to change the world somehow. It's like many in the group just want to give some sort of power-reiki to a person in pain, maybe for themselves to feel good?" Janco watched some sand spill through his fingers before continuing, "But the current system ensures there will just be another thousand in pain within the hour."

Janco walked to the shore to paddle in the edge of the oasis. "I really don't know Sarien, I guess I'm struggling in myself with what to do with this responsibility, and now this new choice on top."

Expecting her to meet his dilemma, confusion, and seriousness somehow, Sarien ran past him naked and dived into the oasis. As he stood in shock, fear, and excitement, Sarien's head rose above the surface with a beautiful smile and shining wet hair, "Stop moaning, come in Janco."

They made love. Taking turns to hold the energy, the male archetype taking care, giving, and overpowering, then the female archetype nurturing, accepting, and nourishing. They knew true tantra wasn't bypassing or blocking the force of creation, as that was just narcissistic quests for self bliss.

They opened all channels they could gracefully open, rising in frequency until their bodies where far below them in the mundane world of dense matter. They could almost see evolved souls waiting to come to earth, but these souls shook their heads, and told them now was not the time, but then the force and energy of creation and love still amplified further until their joint climax pulsed the energy of eternity and unity out from them - where it quickly imploded with force back into them – smacking them back into duality, and physical listlessness.

They laid in each other's arms in the shaded sand. The time that past was unknown nor cared for. Janco knew Sarien had healed his blockage with animals and the nature of the earth, the two areas he'd not touched since his change. She knew *he knew*, and he knew *she knew* he knew.

*

The following months, Janco worked only with those who directly or indirectly hurt the animal kingdom and the earth, meeting with Sarien every two weeks or so.

He visited and healed the leaders, managers, and heads of animal testing laboratories, horse racing stables, whaling operations, dolphin and orca whale theme parks, the dark side of the meat and poultry industry, hunting associations, and mass fishing.

Each time he didn't really seek to show the person bliss and love, he just opened them up and then took them to a place where they themselves could see and feel the pain they were creating, then afterwards smoothed off the spikes in their aura. Each time the person returned from the experience knowing animals were part of the earth family, each with a wisdom trait to teach.

He visited and healed the leaders, managers, and heads of polluting industries, polluting corporations, large landfill operations, fracking executives, utility companies who lied and trampled upon the earth, also loggers, and those involved in damaging the rain forests.

Janco worked relentlessly, and Sarien was there every so often to heal and share, for if it wasn't for her he would have caved in.

It was early February, and Janco took Sarien to a hidden cenote in Oaxaca, Mexico. He had planned for them to spend the day by a large emerald water cave, with a backdrop of a small undiscovered Maya pyramid covered in jungle vines. He even bought along some food from a deli in Paris.

After Janco had etherically blasted all the mosquitoes away (knowing they were manifest forms of low level astral parasites), Sarien shared stories of her recent work. Visits to heads of the western education system, and those that created the left brained curriculum void of any real creativity. Also her visits to human traffickers and those who kept or had a part in slavery. She had come more into Janco's way of thinking, attacking the roots of issues, and not so much the symptoms, but at first it felt strange as only very few in society would know these people needed healing. Most saw these people as simply *bad*, and wanted to lock them in a cage. From Sarien and Janco's level of vibration and insight, these common *thoughts* were toxic, and anyone allowing them through their mind also needed healing.

As they stroked each other's backs amidst increasingly light, humerous, and sweet conversation, Sarien brought up a conversation both had been avoiding.

"So who are you going to choose next month Janco? I've no idea myself whatsoever, but I reckon you'll pick someone special!" Sarien said as she looked into him for clues.

"I just don't know yet Sarien, I've been so caught up in the pain of the animals and earth that it's taken a kinda back seat." Janco looked at her. "You're right, maybe I'll spend the coming time giving this some real intention and thought……today was just what I needed to step back, thanks so much Sarien."

Janco had a look of complete bewilderment with what to do with his choice. At that moment the enormity hit him of the actual power the choice contained, and he committed himself to give all his spare time to making the best possible choice.

"Janco, know I'm here for you, and if it feels good to me, I'm happy to help you when the time comes," Sarien said.

The sun started to lower, and the oranges and browns brushed through the gold rays around the plant life that enshrouded the beautiful ceynote. The jungle pyramid slipped into a dark gold ray.

*

The coming days Janco did work on healing himself, as his new intention had to block out, or at least quieten the pain of humanity, the earth and the animals. It was harder healing himself than others, for he had to go deep into himself and create a new internal canvas to work from; one of health, stability, awareness, and balance.

As he started to deliberate in his front room, he first thought of ascending the least deserving human on the planet, a murdering rapist or similar, as humanity in evolutionary terms was surely only as advanced as its slowest straggler. But he knew the system would just create more, because these traits were symptoms of root causes.

Janco knew society wasn't changing as much as he first thought it would. Soon after he was *changed*, he thought many of the worlds ills would disappear, but though consciousness was changing in individual people, the system that shaped consciousness still held firm. If someone awoke, then others would just replace them. The positions, vacancies, cartels, and mental paradigms still held firm.

Therefore he wanted to chose the ascension state for someone who could have the maximum impact on the current system, one who could make the most drastic and dramatic improvement. Or on the other side of the coin, one that could cease the most toxicity, lessen the most pain.

As he researched, contemplated, and deliberated, in a mix between online research and relaxed meditation, he could feel a tough firm will within himself, a courageous cut throat - almost darkness within him. It sat upon the purity of the motivation to help humanity, the animals, and gaia. Akin to the Buddhist myth where the teardrops of Avalokiteshvara created both white and green Tara, to assist Avalokiteshvara on the path of benefitting all beings.

He wanted to change the *system consciousness* that individual consciousness lived in, or what he did would just be a drop in the ocean.

Politicians, no point, finance men, no point, the Pope, interesting, but again would only be replaced. Police chiefs, no point, Military leaders, no point. CEO's of corporations, no point.

Janco realized most of the ills on the planet were AI, or corporation's prices on the stock markets, or conditioned and engineered mental beliefs. How could ascending one single human change these? How could one person change the capitalistic framework that encouraged greed and competition between men? Or possibly change the communist framework that killed opportunity, free thinking, creativity, and diversity.

He sat for an hour, then another hour. *Hang on*, Janco thought. *Click, read, scroll, click, read, scroll, new tab, search, click, save, click, read, read, read, open, new tab, read, scroll. Hang on a minute*, he thought as he stood up in the singularity of a eureka, "I've got it, I've found my man" he slowly whispered to himself.

Janco danced around his room at the incredulous genius he had found within his eureka, it was perfect. He had a real chance at making real change, and brushed off any notions of overcooking it a bit. He knew it had to be done.

After he had calmed down to a point of being able to converse, he called Sarien telepathically, and she appeared forty seconds later amidst her violet light streaks.

After sharing each of their choices, amidst a fervor of shock, excitement, and questions, they planned that Sariens was to be done at sunrise Greenwich time, and Janco's at sunset Pacific Time.

"You're completely crazy Janco," Sarien said with a grin.

Janco smiled back, "And you're not?" he laughed.

Janco moved towards her to embrace their ideas, courage, love, and delight at finally both knowing their choices were going to create ripples.

*

The Equinox arrived and Janco and Sarien had been separately planning for the weeks beforehand, though meeting up every few days to spend quality time relaxing together, for both needed that to keep their sanity.

Sarien knew it was now post sunrise. The sheet of grey cloud above her had transformed from a dark nothingness to a sterile and rumbling medium grey that went to each horizon. The dated, large, grey palace in front of her looked damp, cold, and unloving, but it riddled in the energy of stature and power. *Here goes*, as she took a deep breath and light-streaked into the right-angled and cold building.

Sarien entered a room empty of people but full of grandeur. Gold chairs, vile garish carpets, oversized portrait paintings of pomp, and ghastly lightshades and chandeliers. *Not here, must be one of the other three rooms*. Sarien light-streaked as quickly as she could into the second living room in the west wing of the Palace.

There she was, the Queen of England, a lone figure walking across the large room of even more ghastly splendor, filled with gold tinted, dark and mid greens. Sarien had to be quick before any alerts where raised, and ran to touch her shoulder as if it was her only aim in the universe.

Immediately Sarien felt the transformative power of sharing and giving raise within the old woman, and a jolt flew a pathway down Sarien's arm. They were both linked within each other, and together linked to a higher energy, an energy of intelligence, wisdom, spiritual knowing and power.

After just four seconds Sarien knew it was done, and pulled away two or so meters, cut all etheric chords, grounded with all the ferocity she could. "Oh my, oh my, what, what have I become, what am I, oh my what can I do?" The Queen blurted out in a pathetic and feeble shake.

"Ma'am, I mean you know harm, you are now ascended in your vessel, a being far different from the one you knew. I really have to go now, so you do what Is right, today! It must be today, and before sunset, then redemption will be yours." Sarien picked a chocolate bourbon from the silver decadent table, and light streaked away back to the oasis in the desert. Sarien jumped straight in to the water to cleanse and rebalance, slowly calming the shaking of her body. As she sunk her head underwater, a big smile started to rise. She started to feel better, and the mischievous smile ceased to fade.

Back in the palace. *Oh my, what a monster I am. The power and control, and the suffering, I felt all the suffering. I have until sunset. What am I to do*, the Queen contemplated. She then told all her aides to leave her alone for the day, save her top aides she could trust, and after an hour of lone time, she gave them orders they needed to follow without telling a soul.

At three in the afternoon the transference of deeds were sent to all corners of the world. Six thousand million acres of land were given back to either their respective countries, nature conservation authorities, homeless charities, poverish families, or orphan groups. A sixth of the planets land mass, with a total value of seventeen billion pounds had been given back.

By three thirty, five hundred small planes started to fly over Africa, Belize, and other countries she had hurt, dropping seeds, small ten dollar nuggets of gold, and small water purification devices.

By four o' clock, the Queen had fallen into a very deep sleep, the energies within her needed to settle.

*

By six o' clock London time, most of the ascended group had chosen a person they loved, a person close to them, or one particular individual in pain, suffering, or despair.

Sarien and Janco were the only ones looking to create real ripples to the roots.

By six thirty the main stream press were still little the wiser to what was going on around the world, but twitter and the forums were starting to spin up with rumors.

*

It was six thirty-two in the early evening (local time) when Janco walked across the sand on Venice beach in Santa Monica, Los Angeles. He felt the sand beneath his feet as he watched the orange sun start to fall quickly towards its destination on the watery horizon.

He knew he had chosen correctly.

He had a second backup choice which was to go to New York to damage Goldman Sachs, the investment banking giant. The backup would be to *choose* their Senior Trading Analyst, and hope he would feel enough pain and gain enough evolved clarity to sell all their positions in the stock markets, and to flitter away any funds into ethical enterprises.

But he knew his first choice had much more potential, and with a last look at the calm waves lapping the sandy beach, he walked inland a few minutes to a hidden alleyway, and light-streaked into a fifth floor office of a nearby large building in the Playa Vista business park.

"What! ….The hell?….Who the hell are you….G..Ga..Gary call security." Craig Delemour shouted at his colleague as he saw Janco materialize within his light-streaks that were now fading.

Janco didn't have time to admire the plush office with a view peering out over the sun beginning to set, he had to act fast. Janco stood still, closed his eyes, invoked, and then in lifting his hands he calmed the room, as if slowing down time. Gary was as if in slow motion, running with a grimace towards the phone, and Janco calmly walked to him, palming his heart at both the front and back, and internally commanded internally with his will, *Calm down, and….ssssleep!*

Time sped back to normal in the visual space, and Gary slumped to the ground in a smiley sleep, and started to dribble.

"Hi, Craig, don't be alarmed, I'm here to help things," Janco said in a friendly tone, whilst sending repellent energy to the otherside of the door so they wouldn't be disturbed.

Craig Delemour was the Software and Innovations manager for ICANN (Internet Corporation for Assigned Names and Numbers), not even a director, or executive.

ICANN was conceived in 1998 by Clinton and Bush, and in 2006 ICANN signed a new agreement with the US governments' Department of Commerce (DOC), which moved the private organisation toward full management of the Internet's system of centrally coordinated identifiers. Basically they manage the whole planets domain names and IP addresses, with the primary principles of operation described as helping preserve the operational stability of the Internet.

Craig was used to firm decisions, and clearly made one to Janco, "I know of your group and what you get up to, I don't know what you want from *me*, but I don't seek any of your crazy cult's enlightenment. I don't seek to be *better* or *happier*, you are meddlers. Now get out."

Janco calmed Craig's energy as he walked slowly towards him, "Enlightenment's a destructive process Craig. It has nothing to do with becoming better or being happier. Enlightenment's the crumbling away of untruth......it's seeing through the facade of pretence....it's the complete eradication of everything we imagined to be true."

Craig was still in astonishment, and Janco stood behind him as the dark red rays of the sun blazed in the window. Janco placed both palms on Craig's shoulders and the *change* began. After twenty or so seconds Janco opened up to higher planes and brought Craig *up* to share in the feelings and vision. They entered the pain created by capitalism, created by central banks, by the stock markets, by investment banks, by the NSA, by the CIA, by the military, and by hedge funds. In the office this went on for only nine seconds, but in the vision they were there for a relative thirty three minutes.

Janco let go, and calmly walked around the desk to sit opposite Craig, who's head had fallen into his hands on his desk. The sun was now beginning to set behind Craig, with a tenth of it falling behind the pacific ocean, and purples hued with orange began to fill the room.

"I....I....I think I know why you chose me.........oh my......I know the framework of the whole system....." Craig said in realisation. He stared at the wall lost in the magnitude of what was possible, then turned to Janco, "What am I to do?....No.......surely not?"

Janco smiled at Craig and whispered, "You can't change the world without crashing the system."

Craig's eyes sparked, as if new life and knowing was born from an inner wave of humility, "I need to wipe the internet, for all it's good, the bad far outweighs it.   Humanity's not ready, it's too dangerous, it creates too much pain, it's in the wrong hands."

Janco had done his research, and needed Craig to be present, "I was hoping you might say something like that Craig. Ok, the root domain service is provided by thirteen servers which exist in multiple physical locations around the world.   Some are sub-managed by Verisign, NASA, the US Military, and RIPE, as I'm sure you know, but we both know *you* can override their systems.   If we manage to disable all the root name servers long enough, the entire DNS system would fail, and the world would be unable to use the internet in any useful manner ever again."

Craig had his new illumination settling slowly, this was due to Janco giving him a big bolt of energy within the change and vision, but allowing the new abilities to slowly drip feed-in over the coming hours, save for the ability of light-streak travel - as Janco knew Craig may need it very soon.

"Yes….yes…..of course.   Ok…er…Janco, come round, watch what I'm doing, I feel a little disorientated so another pair of eyes will help."   Craig knew Janco's name from the etheric sight he now had.

For the next two hours Craig hit keys, loaded scripts, ran batch files, hacked encryptions, ran password and stealth hacks, and worked his way around the central Internet address pools and DNS root registries on the thirteen major servers, much like a playful and graceful - child ballerina.

Janco was out of his depth technically by light years, he knew nothing of the mumbles and mini-eurekas from Craig about IPv4, IPv6, root zones, or top level domains, where each few minutes of key pressing was only interrupted by an abrupt swear word or a mini claim of victory by Craig.

"Janco, this is it, I hit this return key and it all goes bye bye. Even five hundred and twelve other servers surrounding the thirteen will format their own clustered and striped hard drives too." Craig smiled at Janco, and Janco grinned back like a naughty school boy.

"Thanks Janco, welcome to the new world." Craig hit the button, and thousands of mini scripts ran in an inreadable high speed on the two screens for just over a minute, commanding other computers to run their scripts. The first domino had been pushed.

Red lines appeared on another large plasma screen on the wall, a screen that mapped out the status of the Internet's framework. The Internet itself slowly disappeared and effectively removed itself.

The consciousness and system on planet earth was reset in that moment.

All bank accounts were lost, the stock and currency markets disappeared, military weapons systems died, surveillance systems died, email systems died, social media died, retail systems died. The management system for Capitalism died. The system for greed died. But within this action, beautiful places for innovation, creativity, communication, collaboration, and sharing also died. Many airports and hospitals went into a temporary chaos, but the overall benefits outweighed the loss. The pain lessened was more than the pain created.

Injustice anywhere is a threat to justice everywhere, Janco had recently thought when he recently explained his *choice* to Sarien.

Shouting started from nearby rooms, and phones started to ring. There was a knock on the door, "Craig, you have to see this - are you free?"

"Janco, you and I'll have to get out of here, hold on just a few seconds." Craig turned to the door without getting up, and loudly commanded, "Darren, I'm on the phone to the pentagon and CISCO, give me a few minutes." A white lie.

"Janco, I can't thank you enough, just one quick thing, how do I handle this new state, just give me one piece of advice."

"Craig, The Unknown is more vast, more open, more peaceful, and more freeing than you ever imagined it would be. If you don't experience it that way, it means you're not resting there; you're still trying to know. That will cause you to suffer because you're choosing security over freedom....." Janco turned his head back to the door where more knocking was stopped by other voices in the corridor. ".....When you rest deeply in the Unknown without trying to escape, your experience becomes very vast. As the experience of the Unknown deepens, your boundaries begin to dissolve. You realize, not just intellectually but on a deep level, that you have no idea who or what you are. A few minutes ago, you knew who you were—you had a history and a personality— but from this place of not knowing, you question all of that."

They embraced as soldiers would, and both light streaked out of the room. To where each went, the other had no idea. A moment later the Technical Director burst into the room holding a tablet computer that was repeatedly beeping alarm states. He looked around the empty room in as much shock as he had for the multiple red lines on his screen.

*

Janco arrived home to his living room where Sarien was awaiting. They rushed to embrace, holding each other's eyes in the knowledge they had changed the world. As their embrace climbed to increasing movement of their vessels, Shai appeared from nowhere with tiny gold bubbles popping all around him in geometric spirals.

"Janco, Sarien." Shai smiled.

"There was something we didn't tell you in the desert. When the sun sets in the pacific in an hour's time, you and original groups 22's we each chose will all lose your abilities. You will cease to be part of the group. The people you chose will continue for a while, and we will take it from there. Earth needs to rebuild, and we will watch as the new seeds start to sprout. But what you learnt and felt will never leave you. I on behalf of the seven I thank you." He stopped for a while to measure them, to listen to their souls. He smiled at them, bowed, "I go now."

Tiny gold bubbles grew around Shai and when they started spinning he disappeared with a calm look of wisdom and humor.

Janco and Sarien quickly packed some belongings, gemstones, and silver coins, and light streaked for India. To a shack in the northern forests next to a river, one Sarien had secretly been preparing. There they would live simply while giving worship to life, the earth, and higher intelligence.

Entity Tea Time Transformation

They came to everyone, every single soul on the planet; street kids, presidents, nurses, old people's homes, Eskimos, Hedge Fund managers, everywhere, and to everyone.

Each human being on earth received a visit from three entities, all at the same time. If more than one person was in a room, a single person could see only *his* three entities, and no one else's visitors. Obviously they were etheric and working through the inner worlds, having adapted their frequency to appear in this reality, not as physical and dense, but *within* each person, but appearing to their eyes as being outer and external. A feeling, an experience, but not touchable.

The three entities were the same three with everyone, they had split themselves into billions of trios, but like a hive mind they were still connected to the wholesome intelligence of the three living sentient entities. What one person saw, the other people saw, it was not individualised.

First they appeared as angelic beings and spoke softly and gracefully, "It's ok, we have been allowed through into the Earth dimensions quarantine for a few minutes, because the Earth is dying, and this realm is being attacked by dark forces that are eating emotive energy caused by greed, shame, fear, and helplessness….we….."

They appeared to stop in mid sentence, and each human could feel the weight of the collective human consciousness become super present, really being here in the now. A big moment. But why had they stopped? They seemed frozen.

All of a sudden two of them changed to scarier and shorter grey aliens with ray guns. The third still in its angelic form said "No, we decided we weren't to do it like this," The others together said (more like projected than spoke) "Some people are laughing at us, so we need these humans to listen and take notice."

"No, this is not the way, we agreed, come on guys." One of the others changed back to its angelic form.

The one still as a scary grey alien holding a weapon, said, "Nope, I'm staying like this, I have over twenty thousand humans in .....where is it.....hold on.....ah...America, throwing things at me, and many are even shooting fire things at me – I didn't sign up for this!"

The other two seemed to sigh, "Ok, well, we are wasting valuable time, so let's just get on with it."

They then started to look into each human, as if seeing the heaviness of heart, the karma, the pain, the soul story, and then they spoke in unison.

"Each human on this planet will in one minute be given a large dose of what you may know as magic mushrooms, there is no way out of this....it will go straight into your neural and blood systems."

"If you try and refuse you will see the point of my ray gun!" the third piped in.

"Shhhhh.....stop it...I knew you shouldn't have come."

After harsh stares between the three, they in unison continued.

"You will go on a journey for some hours, and we know this is one of only a few possible solutions for your species and planet. Your species is ill in consciousness and that is what is causing your external ills. The inner is linked to the outer, and this you need to learn or else you will wipe yourselves out, or become slaves of dark astral predators. We don't have the man power to setup another Karmic school of evolution, and this one is kind of nice...."

"Yes, those three things they have are incredible, was it Derek from creations involved with them?"

"Will you be quiet, the angelic two said to the scary looking Grey one."   In unison again.

"We will part now, and hope never to return. We love you, you love you."

And with that a massive wave of unconditional love frequency washed over every human being on earth. Babies giggled, bitter old men smiled, and wrinkles fell from them........then the minute was up.

Six billion different journeys started, each person went through their stories, their deep, emotional, soul, creative, and blueprint potential stories.   Some journeys were dark and terrifying, especially for the sociopathic, psychopathic, egoistic, false, manipulative, fearful, and greedy.

For others living in more light, the journey was one of wonder, teachings, and bliss.

After each individuals inner soul journey, all humans rose up etherically to feel the earth, its consciousness, its feelings, and then together with Gaia, the species rose to the sun, then with the Sun, to the galactic centre, then with the Galactic Centre to the whole universe.   Humanity was one in the etheric, love reigned, and all was healed and forgiven......burned away with the forces of love and creation.

The earth consciousness pulsed and the species came down to hover around the earth in a massive ring, each soul in its astral body, and each astral body within the one collective human species' aura, and slowly, the earth aura enveloped that of the human aura, and these auras merged, bonding with love. This lasted many minutes.

Everyone on earth had the same epiphany, the sudden flash and realization that they were indeed all one in essence - every person they ever encountered, an aspect of themselves.   There was no need to harm others ever again as they knew the other they saw was themselves.....just endless forms of I AM... All perfect beings, blemishes and scars and all

Fear of death fell away, as One realized energy itself cannot die.

They knew they were not drops in the ocean, but the ocean in droplets.

Things would never be the same again.

Then with a bit of a thud each soul returned to its own unique physical vessel.

Many of the frail, ill, and elderly did not return to their vessels, it was too much.

For the next few days not much moved on Earth. No cars drove, no airports opened, people just sat in awe, and in love......fear and greed started its dissolution.....and love, grace, and peace started to plant its roots.

Jasper, the Relationship Ghoul

Jasper, the low level astral critter, was scooting about regular haunts in the lower astral looking for scraps of food. Well, more like hunting for dark emotive energy he could feed upon. This was his favourite he told himself, but at his current stage of evolution, he could only handle that of one or two humans at a time. He usually hunted with his friend Claysus, but Claysus had been gone for days, apparently feeding on a single human beings' helplessness and frustration at being in debt, plus the hatred for his boss at work.

Jasper and Claysus would appear differently to different observers due to living in a fast and non physical frequency. To a human who could see the astral plane via the inner worlds, they would appear as smooth smoky clouds, thin and whispy, with the occasional brightness of what may look like red eyes. They were never at rest, always moving, appearing a little like a swarm of flies. Sometimes when in flight or fright mode, these ghoul types would quickly appear spiky instead of curvy, but this was not so common.

Jasper missed Claysus as they often worked as a team, but this time, Jasper all by himself wanted to find some toxic relationship energy to munch on.

It was hard to get in on this act as so many of the bigger and darker ghouls had the handle on this racket, but Jasper was enthusiastic and desperate, especially after his last feed was just that of a poverty stricken and smelly eleven year old boy. A boy whom hated school and nowhere to go energetically but towards disdain and despair. This was because his parents told him fiercely he had to go to school, and *had to do well*. When the boy was at school in complete suffering under the stimuli of boredom and authority, Jasper would slowly whisp into his solar plexus and munch away, usually when the boy was doing mathematics.

But it wasn't a big enough meal, and it was looked down upon by Jaspers boss, the ghoul troll, Winfred.   Jasper knew Winfred was planning his appraisal review soon, and knew Winfred demanded improved results from him, for all the ghouls in the tribe shared to a degree the energy they each fed upon.

At the last round of appraisals, nearly half of Jaspers ghoul tribe were cast out of this frequency to find energy in an even lower world, akin to scouring the bins outside a McDonald's in human terms.   Jasper wanted to impress, if he fed well enough in the coming times, he could even beef himself up into a ghoul troll himself one day, complete with a small army of ghouls working for *him*.   Then he could move into new agers spiritual practices, posing as a benevolent energy and feed away, akin to going to live in Hawaii in an all inclusive five star hotel - in human terms.   But at the moment this remained but a dream to Jasper, but one he floated with as he swooshed around the lower astral.

***

Conka and Shraba had been together eighteen months, they had fallen in lust, flung themselves together, and since had some volatile and passionate ups and downs. They moved in together just after a two months, mainly due to both enjoying the sex and removal from loneliness.   But things had been going downhill rapidly for the past three weeks.

Shraba was insecure, and loved to soak in a drama infused victim-bath.   But her astounding looks and curves gave her power over men, and she knew it. She had used this knowledge since her mid teens as it made her feel more secure when men where in desire of her - it made her feel wanted and beautiful. Her outer beauty looked effortless, but the effort had been done in the past; years of homing this skill now made it near effortless to *look effortless*. In this outer beauty there was an etheric coldness, but most men were too deep in the physical world or appearances and desire to see or pick up on this.

Shraba's left brain was near dormant, she was terrible at logic, organising, maps, and all that sort of thing. She was very right brained, but with years of alcohol and contraceptive pills, her pineal gland, and therefore intuition, was very out of sorts.

Conka was a marketer's dream. He loved technology, football, working at the office, and loved saving for a car modification or a new technical gadget. He recorded all the popular American TV series', read popular men's magazines, and went to the gym. Anything thrown into Conkas subconscious would pretty much stick, and one could say most of his waking being was one big continuous pattern of subconscious reflexes. But he was a good natured person none the less.

They did genuinely care for each other, and oftentimes genuinely laughed together. Their bond found solace and growth in a place where both agreed upon who and what they didn't like, and would share and add reasons why. There were a lot of judgements.

Since they'd moved in together, Shraba had nowhere to go to hide her subconscious insecurities, so they all came out in toxic actions. She had with masterful delicacy cut out Conka'a female friends, and taken control of his wages, wardrobe, and free time. Conka in turn, had become frozen, unable to move or breath, and even a flick through his lads magazine was met with trepidation that was slowly turning into fear.

***

Casper spotted the energy in the distance faintly peaking in and out. Energy shaped with signatures of the ill thought forms of disharmony, restriction, and resentment. This dark red and black mist was spiking in and out of Jasper's home frequency far below, and no other ghouls were to be seen.

If I work this, I could feed for weeks, or even months! Thought Japser with cunning glee.

He knew relationship meals were tricky beasts, one false move and the human couple would simply split up, or go the other way and create unison, bonds, and promises, all sitting upon care and love – and this in-turn would damage Jaspers energy, or could even kill him. He needed to think, plan, and contemplate, but all he could think about was food.

Jasper flew closer and started to study Conka's and Shraba's energy blueprints, as well as the combined relationships aura. Looking for any early entry signals he knew would help him, such as any lacks of attention, acceptance, appreciation, affection, or allowing.   All were slowly becoming more increasingly evident in this union.

Jasper knew many humans searched for an illusory perfect partner for a source of happiness, searching for all needs to be fulfilled, and that humans projected their mental-perfect-partner-archetype onto potential mates. All these traps were evident too with these two.

Human partners in a co-habiting relationship, Jasper knew, was often little more than a business arrangement.   The first encounters would get the endorphins moving, then the image projections of one's *love fantasy* onto the other would occur. Later, when the partner hadn't lived up to the projections, the other would often become angry, and then the food of negative emotions would start to cook.   Jasper also knew one of his enemies, akin to kryptonite, Divine Love, was unconditional love, and if invoked by the partnership, could kill him at a glance.

Jasper groped and stroked the spikes and started to so very gently feed from them. Conka and Shraba started arguing immediately. Intense negative and dark thoughts about each other flew in from the mental plane. This pulsed the spikes and put more dark fractals and flavour into them as Jasper started to feed like a hoard of bats who had been starved of blood for whole lunar cycle. Jasper was now attached to their auras, which were slightly always blended together as they were sexually active together.

He would feed and manipulate as long as he could.

***

The arguments increased. The walk outs, shouting, blame, power and control games, and even vengeance energy popped in at times. Conka was at a loss internally why he was feeling so much resentment, it was as if it was coming from somewhere else. His body would feel tight and stressed, and when he argued it seemed to help his energy release it all. He often pondered where all this energy went.

Yum, yo, yo, yum, slurp, yum, mmmmm, went Japser.

Jasper had to be careful in the coming weeks. When either of them bathed in any natural oils or herbs, or cleaned the house, or even threw rubbish out, he would have to back off a bit.

But he didn't have to go too far away because their apartment always had other etheric food and places for him to hide; toxic TV programmes were always on, and six Wi-Fi and four 4G networks went through the house. Plus the bin was rarely emptied until completely full.

It was time for Jaspers favourite meal, the time of Shraba's menstruation cycle and it was also near the full moon. Menstrual blood, if not kept clean was like a free ticket for Jasper to come super close to the human frequency, and with the coming full moon, the veil was even thinner. From Jaspers view, the sea that the spikes came through would lower so much he could see the outline of the humans, more of their auras, and well, everything, all so much more clearly and accurately.

Mars also had a square to Aries too which would also help with his plan of chaos.

Jasper tipped a thought form into Conka, and then pushed a new thought form into Shraba in the hope of starting an argument. He could get further into Shraba as she had a life pattern of internalising opinions of others, and then twisting them externally to make her a appear a victim.

They went at it for hours; shouting, blaming, vengeful threats, ignoring, not listening, hurting, and overpowering the other. Black fractals flew out of each of them, even ancestral and childhood crud was invoked and pulled through them into the argument.

Yum, yo, yo, yum, slurp, yum, mmmmm, went Japser, as he shooed away smaller less evolved critters attached to the sanitation in the toilet bins who thought to get a free feed.

As the anger, pain, sadness, expectations, and blame increased, Jaspers realm was evoked even closer to their auras, and in-turn he could manipulate their thought forms towards even more darkness.   Jasper could drag negative thoughts down for each of them, and then add to them, and then pull them together into one shared *mind virus* that sat in the mental plane, but impeached into each of their auras.

Conka started to even get images of violence, they appeared in the top right of his forehead curving around in a thin arc to the back of his head.   But he held his rage at the level of loud abuse.

Shraba lost control and threw plates at him as they merged into one thought form verging on hatred.

"I wish I never met you!" Cried Shraba.

"Me neither, you're ruining my life" replied Conka.

"Then leave, and never come back" Shraba threatened.

"That's the only useful thing you've said in the last month," Conka retorted with a hiss, and packed his things and stormed out with a slam of the door.

***

For the coming days Shraba sat listless and empty in the apartment, still heavy with the energy from the volcanic argument. But she was not so much empty because Jasper was inside her aura munching away like a medieval king on a chicken drumstick. She felt justified in being angry with Conka, and after the third day of sulking and brooding, her body became so exhausted she went to bed late afternoon.

In the reverie-state just before sleep, she dwelled once more on all her troubles and sorrows, and on the one who had angered her. Jasper feasted until sunrise.

The next morning when she awoke, her mind was still occupied with much the same situation. Her bodily vitality has been partially restored and the body was charged with new vitality. But as soon as the image of her archetypal enemy returned, the burning pain of everything that kept her anger alive flowed into her emotional being. And with his new vitality she wasted it in future mental projections of responses, retorts, and blame leverage if Conka was to communicate with her this day.

Consequently, upon awakening in that state, she was prepared again for the fight. The same struggle started anew and the enmity returned.

*

Conka had gone to a friend's place who was away, and had attempted to calm himself in the large tree lined garden.

Japser had munched upon Conka in the first two days since he left, but then slowly started to feel Conka's energy slip away from him. For the time being Jasper had enough to feed on with Shraba and the apartment so didn't mind. The apartment had a fog of dark energy hanging around, like a morning mist rising from the trenches of an old war.

***

Conka felt a lot better in himself three days later, like a weight had lifted, but he still felt sad for Shraba and the damage done to their relationship. But when he thought of her and their relationship more deeply, it was as if negative and dark thoughts came into his mind, and then he felt tired afterwards, less like himself.

Yum, yo, yo, yum, slurp, yum, mmmmm, went Japser, as Conka's aura was in reach once more.

Jasper's was finding it easy to wait in and around Shraba's aura for she was in a desperate state, verging on vengefulness and hatred. He was, one could say, twenty percent the way towards a full possession, but Jasper didn't have the knowhow or the power to commence such a skilful task. Winfred was the only ghoul he knew that had been able to do this, and that was only one time.

Conka on the other hand was feeling more clear, and was in more of an upset and caring state, a wanting to pick up the pieces. He loved her soul, but somehow felt it had been eaten up. Conka woke with renewed positivity and sent Shraba a facebook message attempting to clear the air, in which he apologised, opened up, and spoke about them needing some space.

Jasper had got stronger in the apartment, and could enter into the electrical system, and even feel any auric energy that came into the apartment through ethernet, 4g, or Wi-Fi.

As this message opened on Shrabas laptop, Jasper held and twisted the auric feel of the message, and tugged it into Shrabas aura, as he also himself input negative thought forms into shraba. Shraba read the message through a filter of resentment, she picked up on none of the positivity, and filtered anything neutral down into negativity.   The soft request for some space was met with insecurity, disdain for the past, and fear of the future. She typed without thinking, hitting each key, forgetting to separate paragraphs;   blame and victimisation led the assault as she attacked, aiming to hurt him, aiming to bring him down to her level of pain and desperation.

Yum, yo, yo, yum, slurp, yum, mmmmm, went Japser, as Conka's aura was in reach once more.

For the coming days this continued, a couple of days of feeding, and as the feeding lessened, a new text, email, or facebook message would commence some dialog that Jasper could twist — increasing the energy to feed upon.   It was a big meal, and Jasper just needed to keep their auras intermingled in the astral plane.

Conka started to see the pattern. *It's as though parasites are attached to the resentment she's firing at me,* he thought as he sat in the woods near his friends house.   *I'll text her that I seek no contact for a while, we need space from all contact.*

Conka started to spend more time alone in the woods in the coming days. He realised that embracing his silence was a brave way to deal with stress, especially at a time he just wanted to yell. It meant he wasn't afraid to sit with his own anger for a while, and face it, hear its message out.   With no one to blame or hold accountable for him, but himself.

It's so easy to lash out and project fears and anxiety to the world around me, but it's always hard to take time out to do some introspection, observe what's deeply rooted in me, why my emotions are ignited, what triggers the pain, and why I can't live with it.

Conka slowly got to a state where he could now clearly and objectively see the relationship with Shraba was based on toxic foundations.   Without her aura entwined with his from cohabiting, or the lure of sexual acts , he was cementing into himself once again, and able to see purely through his *own* eyes and energy.

She was too volatile, her words meant little, she was a scared little insecure girl with masks upon masks, with the consciousness always on how she and they appeared to others externally. It was false, toxic. He realised neither of them had any control over their individual personalities, and that they had no desire to either. But these were stepping into far out thoughts, *maybe too much time in nature and solitude*, he mused.

Conka found more realisations in the coming days from his contemplations.

Grief's favourite position is piggyback. If I'm abandoned in the present and allow myself to grieve the abandonment, all the old abandonments of the past, which have been waiting their turn, jump onto my grieving shoulders.

Conka started to reminisce much of what his late father had taught him when he was younger. Conka had ignored him those years ago, but was willing to delve into anything to heal this pattern somehow.

***

More days in the woods brought more peaceful thoughts, *Peace is already here, it is within me, in front of me, I only need to be in touch with it. I do not need to chase it. The act of chasing is only wasting my energy and confusing me, and taking me away from peace.*

Some of the things that look bad and destructive might actually be needed to pave way for the new.

Letting go can prove to be more helpful, even life saving, than grasping at toxic strings, looking for what ifs or chasing disillusioned beliefs.

Energy vampires usually tend to be heavily identified with the victim persona, and they use guilt strategies to manipulate, and they love for other people to feel pity for them – for this is how they get their energy.

The abusive texts and messages kept coming in, but Conka now had enough courage to forgive her for hurting him, and to forgive himself for allowing her to hurt him. It was time to close this chapter in his life. Preparation was required.

Yum, yo, yo, yum, slurp, yum, mmmmm, went Japser, as he had nearly forgotten about Conka as he ravenously fed on Shraba's energy.

*

It was full moon, and Conka knew Shraba went to her friends every Wednesday after work. He had time. After a salt scrub then a chamomile herb bath, he used his key to enter their shared apartment. It felt heavy and sad.

Jasper was sleeping in the electric humming and electric chill of the refrigerator, but woke to Conka's energy. Jasper started to feel ill, Conka was strong, he could in no way feed off him, just Conka's presence was starting to hurt him. Jasper went into the freezer compartment at the top of the fridge next to some old mince, he would be safe here, especially next to mashed pigs ears and genitals.

Conka started to cleanse the apartment; first lighting tea-candles in each room that floated on a bowl of spring stream water with lavender. Then he smudged the each room with burning sage and rosemary, giving special care to the corners of each room whilst whispering some Hebrew softly.   He then sat in the middle point of the apartment, and once in deep stillness of his meditation, he infused light into each room.

Arrrghhh, went Jasper, *Nooooo, I must stay in this frequency, where is Shraba? Argghhhh*.   Jasper mooched closer to the mince, to be more cosy to the pain energy of the pigs lives, and the pain in their butchered deaths.   It was his only place of solace as the apartment became engulfed in a higher frequency, one which Jasper could not live in without serious injury.

Conka then opened all the windows whilst he collected his belongings, then closed the windows, placed a letter about parting, finance and logistics on the bed, and then left.

Conka then returned to his dwelling, and started a three day alkaline juice fast.

On the final day of his fast Conka worked with the medicine Buddha mantra, and performed a small humble ritual of forgiveness and renewal, letting go of Shraba without expectation, fear, censure, blame, shame, or control.

Once in meditation, he imagined a long chord attaching himself to Shraba, and with a big out-breath he pulsed a wave of love and forgiveness from his heart - this beamed along the chord towards her. When it hit her the chord cut and dissolved, and she flew into the horizon as she shrunk.

Conka had moved on.   He was now adamant he wouldn't ever again let her walk through his my mind with her dirty boots.

The next day Conka contemplated intimacy and love in a new light.

It's a different thing, to make a relationship sacred. When it's just the love you honour, you're still in two different worlds. You love her, she loves you, but what stands between you? What of the bridge between your hearts? What of the world you become together? Conscious relationship is all about the third element- the alchemical combination of two souls merging, the world that you co-create in love's cosmic kiln. It's the difference between loving and serving love. It's the difference between the narcissistic quest for ecstasy and the joys of deep devotion. You serve loving. You are a devotee to the dance. Love is the capacity to take care, to protect, to nourish. If you are not capable of generating that kind of energy toward yourself- it;s very difficult to take care of another person. Love is a practice.   I won't look for the right partner, I'll become the right partner, then the right partner will find me.

*

A few weeks later Jasper was a little stronger than when he had the dangerous encounter of Conka's last visit.   But he was still feeding off Shraba and living in the apartment.   Shraba had started going out and having one night stands to suppress the pain, and in this energy of lack and giving ones body through insecurity, Jasper could feed once more

On the whole, Winfred would be most pleased.

Holistic Revolution Flip

By 2026 the Management Artificial Intelligent system (known as MAI, or Mai to most), had grown to unprecedented proportions.

It now controlled the stock markets, currency markets, interest rates, inflation, bail-outs, treasury bonds, the food supply chain, medicine, hospitals, housing, austerity, energy, utilities, the education system, financial transactions, transport systems, and even had Humans PLC floating as a stock. The new stock of Humans PLC was given a floating number so that MAI could see the human populations' potential and trajectory for future growth, but many thought it was for measuring human obedience in the increasingly electronic totalitarian system. A system which still masqueraded as a type of warped democratic capitalism.

Google had brought Facebook, Twitter, News Corp, and Time-Warner in 2018 and then launched MAI in 2020 without much media fuss. Apple had by then brought most large banks and franchise stores once its transaction and supply chain systems went online in 2019. Things spiralled from there, and by 2026, the world was pretty much run by MAI acting as an umbrella over Google, Apple, and Goldman Sachs (GAG), who together had one group of Directors and Executives which floated between each of the three boardrooms.

It was an illusion of three competitive conglomerates working underneath politicians, with a puppy dog AI for administration, but the reality was far different, and over ninety percent of the people knew it. Politics had become no more than voting for different spokesman of GAG based upon their personality or life stories, and the most recent voting turnout was only twenty three percent.

Hartman was on his way to another protest, and eyed with disdain a group of rich types getting off the tube as he boarded. Both men had expensive suits on, and four girls were in tow, following them in quick tiny steps, each with fake hair, eyelashes, boobs, nails. These rich decadent types made their money supporting GAG and were rarely seen on public transport these days. Probably due to the disdain aimed at them from the ever increasing poverty class.

As Hartman boarded the carriage his Goog-ALL pinged into his vision twenty centremeters from his eye and the half opaque screen appeared, *Hartman, £18 has been deducted from your APPLE-1 Account for this journey, blink twice for safety advice.* Then an advert showing a weekend trip to Bordeaux he would never want, let alone afford. It played for twenty seconds and he knew he couldn't stop it as it was part of the electronic sponsoring of the tube trains.

Profile advertising had technically worked for a few years a while back, but had died once GAG gobbled up the last standing corporations and companies.   GAG now showed everyone what they wanted to sell, regardless of who they were or what their status was.

Hartman sat down and saw graffiti scrawled on most of the platform billboards that were each advertising the latest gadgetry chips or virtual reality dating clouds. His Goog-ALL was old, but he didn't desire an upgrade, he was even thinking of getting rid of this one, but GAG had made it hard to live, move, identify oneself, or even pay for anything without a chip from their recent product range. Hartman touched the small metal device stuck behind his ear, and as he tweaked it a red circle appeared in his vision and started to blink *Warranty Alert, Please Refrain from Chip Movement.*

GAG the Slag Hag Sh1tbag, The first graffiti scrawled. The second he saw as the tube smoothly pulled away stated, *All on a screen = toxic, all in a packet = toxic. The Time is now, HOL1ST1C is coming.* The third one was hard to read as the tube sped up, but Hartman twisted his neck and focused his eyes to catch all the words, *Don't try and bend the government, That's impossible. Instead, only try to realize truth. There is no government, only GAG.*

Hartman turned his focus back to the carriage, and could see others texting or watching something. Their eyes were glazed, as if they were looking at something or someone who wasn't there in front of them. With the newer chips one could think the words onto the screen, but since these became popular, Hartman noticed emotion and personality was on the decrease in public places. People weren't present anymore in the environment they were actually having a real experience.

The very latest chips could also record what one was seeing and hearing at any time, and share with others such as partners, friend groups, or even live stream to GooTube. This had already started to be hacked, most notably a celebrity singer who was known for drugs and sex had her whole weekend put online. She was now under medication in a clinic and had become the current fashionable source of ridicule.

The new chips could also give profile information, including photos, likes, and life timeline of anyone they looked at (triggered by blinking then looked right-up quickly), as long as the one being viewed had their sharing turned on. Many lived by what had became fashionably known as *chip-commando*, thinking it cool to have all their details open to everyone.

As the tube neared Camden, more people going to the protest got on board. They were those who knew humanity lived in a locked-down and forced-poverty, where expression was quashed. Many of them had changed in recent years too, for just a couple of years ago the protests were formed by mostly online-cloud-junkies, hackers, and people with an anti feeling of anger, but nowadays the masses at the protests were more holistic.   Those that grew food away from GAG, those who lived in any way apart from the grip of GAG's control, those who sought another more holistic way.

Floyd got on the tube at the stop before Camden, and Hartman got up to greet him. Floyd could tell what carriage Hartman was on using a GoogAll *Friend Location* app, pretty much the norm since two decades ago.

"What do you think Floyd?" Asked Hartman, as Floyd blinked at an app to stop some music.

"I think this one tonight's a bit different Hartmann.   Since HOL1ST1C's grown in popularity allot recently, I think they'll seize the moment and launch a *real* type of movement tonight." Floyd brushed his fringe out of his eyes, and swept back his blonde pony tail in some sort of physical readiness.

Hartman was shorter and stockier than Floyd, and with darker brown-black hair. He looked quite tough from a distance but was really more of a soft bear. Floyd on the other hand was lean and nimble, always super alert and impatient looking.

"How many you think are coming?" Asked Hartman.

"They said on the *hackhush* channels that at least ten thousand might be there," Floyd raised his eyebrows, and then nodded a few times in a readiness jig, as though he was going to a rave...or enter battle.

Hartman didn't use the *hackhush* channels, and tried as much as he could to use as little tech as possible.

Hartman worked with Floyd sometimes in the large industry called *The Rounds,* where people in the poverty class worked on a variable-rota with menial jobs such as cleaning streets, or security and automation controlled; GAG administration, GAG distribution, or GAG supply chain.

Workers in *The Rounds* received no usable cash but instead received online GAG credits which were nearly all auto-allocated for tax, food, rent, and utility payments. It was seen by GAG as a generous welfare system controlled by MAI, but in reality it was slavery as it was compulsory. Those that chose to leave *The Rounds* ended up on the streets, or became stim-junkies, or became freaks in the digital entertainment parlours and dens.

*

Thousands were already walking up to the massive old warehouse in Camden as Hartman as Floyd entered the flow and direction of the hoards. Two drone-copters flew overhead underneath the darkening haze of pollution and grey cloud, and every now and then from the front of the warehouse they could hear a megaphone repeating the same command:

PLEASE TURN OFF ALL LOCATION AND RECORD SETTINGS ON YOUR CHIPS AND GADGETARY BEFORE ENTERING.

A few years ago protests were banned, but this caused some voilent riots, and from a year ago protests were again allowed as long as they had permission. GAG wanted to appear as democratic, and as a promoter of free speech, but always kept a beady eye on large gatherings, and kept most protests out of the media.

Upon entering, a scanning device above the large open doors scanned for recording or surveillance equipment, and once inside Hartman could see chrome pods every ten metres or so, high on the walls, obviously trapping and blocking any monitoring, location, or recording gadgets.

He and Floyd both looked around, it must have been nearer twenty thousand in there, and at the front stage the large digital green logo of HOL1ST1C provided the backdrop. Hartman spent a moment to ponder how holistic it was to have a three metre digital screen, but let it pass as some movement on the stage began.

Most of the people there knew of the charismatic Halo, the creator of HOL1ST1C and very much its mouthpiece. Halo was a yogi, a raw foodist, an empathic, and had self proclaimed states enlightenment. He had the look of a confident model, and silence fell across the waves of people as he took to the platform.

"We all know…….we *all know*, and that is why we come. That is why we have had enough!" Halo beamed, then nodded his head.

Large cheers resonated through the warehouse.

"We are forced to eat crap, to live in an electronic grid, to be controlled by a system where not one atom is from stardust, where not one atom is from source. And we know, we saw it, the old high-streets died, the stores died, family business' died, our communities died, but now, but now my friends, it is the time to fight back, to fight for our naturaaaal freeeeeeeedooooom."

More cheers and shouts of allegiance boomed out from the audience.

"Many, so many……..many thought this system would have died out around 2015, or 2016, but here we are, all the way in 2026….and still it tightens its grip. But tonight we tip the balance. Tonight we level the playing fiiiieeeeeeeeeld."

A hush and apprehensive excitement fell upon the hoards.

"Our expert and talented hacking team have been at work, and they have created a device we give to each of you tonight. This device will increase your GAG credits to any number you want and will not raise any flags, it will also nullify any drone or GAG device within thirty metres. We will update the devices remotely with patches in the near future too.   Please, each of you, each of you who desire freedom, take one now, and do what yoooou neeeeeeed.   We will meet here again in one week.   Let it staaaaaart toniiiiiiiiiiiight!"

About a hundred men dressed in black marched in pairs through the crowd, each delivering large boxes full of small chrome devices, not dissimilar to the very first mobile phones. They were crude, but if what Halo said was true, the crowds would use anything to give them just an ounce of more freedom.

Hartman looked at it, it had a small green screen and just an arrow keypad, old tech for sure, crude, and obviously cheap for mass production. The small menu system allowed for the deactivating of GAG devices, or the increasing of GAG credits, it was cumbersome to use, and Floyd turned to Hartman and whispered, "This is a game changer, this will cause chaos my friend, needed chaos, but some very real chaos."

Before Hartman could reply, Halo continued from the stage, "We are also working on a hack for MAI, she has her pants down, and we are walking slowly to the bedroom. We have made some progress but need more time, and hopefully next week we can tell you more. Now go my friends, and without violence or anger, for that is how the Statists solve their problems, go, and push theee fiiiirst dominooooo!"

Cheers and yells of revolution filled the warehouse as the crowds started to leave.

Hartman and Floyd were three quarters to the back and as they exited the warehouse there seemed to be a hold up ahead, then shouts from ahead, and then a surge from the crowds behind.

Three O-Drones sped in to the exiting crowds from above, and hovered thirty metres in the air in a triangle - about thirty metres from the entrance. Black and Spherical, each with five red lights blinking at different rates, and each about two metres in diameter. They started to hum, which was preparing for aggression or the capturing of personal information.

Hundreds of arms raised in the air from the crowd at the front who had exited first, each with a silver extension from their hands. Thumbs pressed in unison with harmonic emotion. The drones dropped with gravity to the ground and smashed into hundreds of pieces.

Cheers and roars swept through the crowds as their exit became a stampede, one of victory, of freedom, of excitement.

In the next thirty minutes around the warehouse, another thirty or so O-Drones were destroyed.

Most of the crowds had left within an hour, but a hardcore right hundred stayed seeking to take out as many drones as they could, to revel in their newfound unity.

About six years ago in 2020, most of the military and police had been dismantled. MAI and GAG had efficient systems for complaints, violence, theft, crime, and disturbance, and even had further more systems for prevention and pre-control. If needed, punishments were via GAG credit fines, or by being taken away by the GAG secret police without notice. MAI and GAG had put most of its faith in electronic control, allowing funds that woul've been spent on manpower to instead be spent on gaining control of more nations, and their systems or infrastructure. For this is how she grew.

Courts and lawyers were disbanded in 2022 as evidence was rarely debatable due to surveillance technology, and MAI was deemed to calculate judgements far more efficiently than any jury could.

The eight hundred or so around the warehouse were half expecting a mass of riot police to turn up, but they didn't exist anymore, it was as if MAI was unsure of what to do.

Soon, a black militarised bus steamed up the concourse to where the remainder of the hardcore group were cheering and dancing. Out of the bus marched twenty or so humanoids with AppCop logos on their uniforms, and masked with black visors.

The crowd's silver devices beeped, and the small green screens flashed: *Upgrade Update, Deactivation Functionality Increased.*

The eight hundred or so each pointed their silver devices at the twenty or so AppCops and pressed the buttons with an emphasis of their will, with all the thumb strength they could muster.

The AppCops all slumped to the floor like rag dolls.

The eight hundred strong crowd ran in different directions and disbanded, with the odd drone swooping down towards one or two stranglers, only to soon slump to ground with a crash.

*

Hartman had lost Floyd in the crowd.

After the fourth O-Drone had fallen, two more came swooping in at high speed, and their small group of sixty or so around the side of the warehouse had ran in different directions. Hartman closed his front door and sighed, as if the sigh itself pushed all the crazyness out of his home. He then pondering how even in times of unity and camaraderie, man can quickly jump into an *everyman for himself* type mode.

Hartman stood under a silver H-pod on the ceiling until it beeped, this was a hacking device that shut off all internet packets in or out of his apartment, and then went to water the plants on his roof terrace.   His vegetables and herb garden was not doing great, mainly due to the poor water he was feeding them, but he found solace here, away from the world of digital control, a world that he longed would end.   From the roof some roars and shouting could be heard, then what sounded like a car crash, and then the small hum of some O-Drones travelling at speed.   *The crazyness has already started,* he thought. *All I want's a quiet life, and to live a more natural life......but......hey....wait a minute..*

It didn't take long before Hartman was back on his roof terrace, sat tapping his thumb lightly over a button that would add six hundred and twelve credits to his GAG account.   *Is this too much? Is this not enough? Is this inconspicuous enough?*

This was around a week's pay for one of the decreasing rich class, and Hartman presumed others within the twenty odd thousand would have typed in as many zeros as possible.

Click.

What now?   Hartman thought as he half expected O-Drones to swoop down, or his GoogAll to kick in and present a warning or crime-tab.   Nothing.

Best get rid of it and spend it, and if caught, I can say it was stolen or something.

Hartman turned off his H-pod and then spent all the new credits on superfood powders and on one of the best water filtration systems. They were two things that would give him and his plants more vitality, something all those who supported H0L1ST1C knew to be important.

Hey, how could I get caught anyway?   If any O-Drone came here I would just knock it out, He thought.

Within the hour a small unintelligent delivery drone swayed and wobbled a metre from the ground of his roof terrace. It beeped, and let go of its claws holding the packages. Hartman was delighted, to obtain such things always seemed a fantasy, a daydream, but H0L1ST1C had done it, they'd found a way.

*

In the coming days the momentum of the movement increased. More drones were destroyed by the devices, and small groups went on the rampage destroying GAG properties and surveillance devices. Looting took place at GAG warehouses and people were on the streets in celebration.

But this was only one result of the crude H0L1ST1C device, one that was now being sold, replicated, and customised in some parts of the city. GAG credits, which were always from the start backed by nothing tangible like land or commodities, were flooding into the electronic economy. Delivery drones filled the sky as around twenty thousand accounts now had extra credits. The automated supply chain surged, the markets surged, and MAI, the only intelligence able to rebalance the mess, was being subtly hacked, as if a small anaesthetic pin was gently prodding into her, sedating her without her knowledge.

The majority bought seeds, water filtration systems, materials, and tools with the credits, and only a few percent slipped into decadence – those buying gadgets and products that effectively supported GAG. This small percentage outwardly supported H0L1ST1C, but their subconscious minds had been so bombarded over the years that their desire pangs were no longer their own.

The city was becoming free of GAG control, revolution was rising, people were on the streets, and AppCops and O-Drones were nowhere to be seen. None of the ninety or so percent that sought change went to their work placements, for they had extra or even unlimited credits – whether sourced from themselves or a friend with a device. Vegetable gardens and fruit trees were planted in city parks, surveillance technology was destroyed and defaced. Yurts and domes popped up in the parks and a festival feel was born, a feeling that sat upon a glimpses of freedom.   People shared stories while eating organic food, food that they would never have been able to afford before, and the delivery drones continually buzzed to and from the parks, bringing more items they needed, and most were now hosting graffiti with their new name; H0L1ST1C Flyer.

Hartman had spent an hour at one of the parks, taking it all in and eating some tofu and qinoa with a group of people, of which he knew only Floyd.   Another H0L1ST1C Flyer swooped down and delivered some smoothies.   The crowds cheered and stroked the flyer as a pet, one adding some dreadlocks to it, creating much laughter from the group.

"But how holistic is a flying drone?" Asked Hartman to the group of nine, alarming himself that his thought came out aloud.

Floyd gave him an icy stare, and the girl who was obviously with the large alpha male in the group piped up.

"What you on about? You're eating the food I see! Do you miss your fear based reality? Do you want to fuck off back to the five percent and back to *The Rounds*?

"That's not what I meant….I meant-" Hartman was broken off.

"No pessimist ever discovered the secret of the stars, or sailed to an uncharted land," the large male said. He stood up, and only when everyone was looking at him did he continue…

"While the leaders of GAG unite for control, some little people like you are busy moaning instead of uniting. GAG has been pillaging the planet and the people, but you are all too worried about silliness and can't see the forest for the trees….and you can take that somewhat literally since your forests are being cut and you don't even have a clue."

Everyone in the group turned their heads towards Hartman, as if grabbing the energy of the man's words and pointing them in his direction with amplification.

"Steady on, I only said th-" Hartman said.

"Yeah, yeah, only this, only that. Go find somewhere else to sit." The girl said.

Hartman walked off with a bad taste brewing inside him, he could not pinpoint it yet, but something didn't sit right.

His GoogAll flashed up, it was a message from Floyd. *"You ok buddy? I understand where you were coming from, but now's not the time bud. I'm going to stay a while, but see you soon. F"*

*

That night twelve people died. *The Festival Parks of Purity* as they had become known were attacked by O-Drones, and the chrome devices didn't work. MAI must have upgraded and patched the O-Drone's firmware. This was far from expected because it was know by the crowds that HOL1St!C was hacking MAI. The O-Drones swooped down and chose one to come with them (in this the person would be locked into a pale-red magnetic field below the O-Drone to walk the path they set out). The crowds nearby then stepped into the pale red field around the person to mess with the O-Drones sensors. This was something someone wouldn't have done before due to profiling and a new crime-tab, but the revolution was in full swing and these people had already gone too far to return.

Then ten AppCops ran into the park in some hard coded formation of aggression. Again the devices didn't work, and after some commands and threats by the AppCops were jeered at, all hell broke loose.

Two of the AppCops started shooting, and then the O-Drone which was capturing someone wooshed up vertically for four metres, stopped, then suddenly crashed down on top of the person.

The o-Drones and Appcops had been upgraded.

As the screams and terror whipped up to a frenzy, the silver devices beeped, and the small green screens flashed: *Upgrade Update, Deactivation Functionality Increased.*

After a few more seconds, the AppCops and O-Drones crashed to the ground, nullified, but the O-Drone sat still, half deep into the earth.....with a bloody arm poking around the curvature of its lower hemisphere.

The park mostly disbanded in chaos, save for those who stayed to cover and help the bodies of the deceased. But as word got around, all the other *Festival Parks of Purity* remained open and crowded as an act of defiance.

In the coming days the *The Festival Parks of Purity* grew and grew, and MAI slowly came to be more under H0L1ST1C's control. Those at the parks knew the delivery drones products were finite and something would have to change soon, but this was never mentioned, probably because most were looking to H0L1ST1C's next gathering for direction and information.

*

Hartman and Floyd met up to go to the meeting together, which was to be held in the largest *Park of Purity.*

"But Floyd, how *pure* is getting electronic drones to deliver automated products?" said Hartman, more in a statement than a question.

"Hartman, that sort of talk won't get us anywhere, we've pretty much toppled the system, it's a time for celebration and fun. I'm sure after tonight we'll know more."

There must have been over forty thousand people at the park. At the front was a stage with two large video screens either side, and more large screens dotted further back, each showing the logo of H0L1ST1C. Above the stage about twenty metres hovered three O-Drones draped in vines and plant-life.

Halo sprang onto the stage with is arms raised in victory. The adulation swept throughout the park.

"Are you with uuuuuus?" He, paused, then when everyone's eyes were on him, he repeated twice as loud.

"Are you with uuuuuuuussss?"

"There are still a few that are not with us. But those few don't give a shit because they are so deluded by their celebrity, shopping, vacations, and whatever other bullshit that has distracting them away from the fact.

The fact that without this natural planet they have nothing. To those not with us I would ask, have you distinguished the difference between having been sold a lie, and having brought a lie, because there's all the difference in the world attitudinally between those two statements. You *are* being sold a lie! But that's the perfect right of GAG to sell you a lie.

To those who are not with us yet, know this - Whatever can be threatened, whatever can be shaken, whatever you fear, is destined to crash. Do not go down with the ship. Let that which is destined to become the past slip away. Believe that the real you is that which beckons from the future. If it is a sadder you, it will be a wiser one. And dawn will follow the darkness sooner or later. Rebirth can never come without death."

Halo paced for a while within the grand silence, and in this he whipped up more energy for the next part of his speech.

"When imagination is put on hold, a society of good people dies. It can look like many other causes are producing the decline and fall, but at bottom it's the lack of imagination. That's why societies go into the swamp. But *we* have used our imaginations, and the fruits are now growing. Peel the skin and taste the fruits………"

Cheers filled the void of the pause.

"We've now got control of MAI, we don't fully understand her yet, but she is ours. And as for GAG? GAG had less people at the top than we first thought, and they have now run and disbanded. Gone are the psychopaths that cared only for comfort, control, and power. GAG was mainly just an automated electronic system in the cloud, so now we have MAI, and she's coming around to our way of thinking."

The three O-Drones above Halo then swooped down to sit a meter to either side and above him. Then he extended his arms and pointed his fingers forward in victory, and all three darted above the heads of the crowds to the far end of the audience. They flew, swooped, and danced their way back to Halo's side, for him to pet them.   They bobbed up and down as if purring and requesting more pets from their new master.

"We've changed the name of MAI, for we will need her in this coming time. We need a new system in place. The parks have been great, but they're not sustainable. For this new rebirth of humanity, we've given MAI her new name, HAL, Standing for HOL1ST1C Attitudes Live.

All the screens in the large park changed from a feed of Halo to a digitised Elf princess, and the same feed appeared on everyone's GoogAll type gadget.

Hi I'm HAL, now GAG has gone and MAI has gone, I am with HOL1ST1C and you, for a better more sustainable world. I love you.

Hartman felt a little dizzy, he looked around and could feel a small percentage being a little stunned by all this, not sure how to take it all in. But in all, the masses cheered and whooped, and wolf whistled, and this brought many of those in confusion into the fervour of the group.   The pain of GAG had created so much despair and disdain that most were still in a wild celebration.

*

Hartman and Floyd stayed in the park for the wild party of celebration. Music played to the tribal dancing, and kava-kava (a superfood stimulant from Fiji), provided the hedonistic outlet.

As the waxing moon filled the sky, Hartman turned to Floyd as they rested by one of the many fires.

"How do you think this will pan out Floyd?   I thought they would've disbanded MAI and the drones?"

Floyd shrivelled his face up in disgust.

"Hartman, you must be the most negative person in this whole park! Halo's a great man, and we need HAL as he says, we need to rebuild and use what we have for better lives, not to go back to the times of the caveman. What is it you seek Hartman, do you want to go back to *The Rounds*?"

Hartman stared deeply into the flames, almost through them.

"Floyd, I just seek authentic freedom, with no masters above, and no slaves below."

Before Floyd could reply, Hartman got up and walked through the celebrating masses, and the litter, and strolled home to sleep.

*

Three months later things were on more of an even keel.   The parks were now permanent and functioning spaces for workshops, schooling, yoga, meditation, carnivals, trading, and food. HAL was providing electricity, transport, and clean water freely to the people. The O-Drones were still in service but mainly used for deliveries, plus also keeping a presence in some areas where looting and theft had continued, but they were yet to be used in any aggressive way.

People kept their properties, and new innovative ideas were launched from a mixture of HAL, Halo, and the people – creating conduits where people could apply energy – a form of *work* if you like (but the word *work* was never used). The people still used their chips and gadgets to communicate and surf the internet, and this was becoming a more collaborative place of sharing ideas and presenting useful information to help people.

The credit system still existed but was changing, people now received credits from HAL based on good deeds, showing compassion, or applying energy to something useful,   wherein they received no personal reward. This system controlled by HAL was in its infancy, and had its teething problems, but was already much loved by the populous. The HAL credits were still used for purchasing food, properties, clothes, and other items, but it was thought that the HAL Credit system would evolve past these transactions given time and support.

Vegetables and fruit trees were planted throughout the city, and a H01ST1C led project for art, colour, and beauty swept through the streets.

A utopia was being born, and the people were celebrating and taking part……….well, mostly.

There were still hackers creating and moving illegal credits, people stealing other people's online profiles, and those who didn't participate. There were those who opened what would have been illegal bars for alcohol and narcotics, and new shops appeared for processed food and sweets, and much of this fell into a grey area that for the time being, HAL had left alone.

On one Saturday evening a disturbance occurred in one of the new club-bars called *The Old Den*. It was really a hedonistic rave in one of the suburbs near the pleasure-cloud dens and hacker cafes, and was growing in popularity. The rave ran nonstop from Friday night till Monday morning, and was becoming a dwelling for those not fully into the H0L1ST1C vibe but loved their new freedom. They had no love for GAG and enjoyed the new freedom, but were just not a part of the yogi, super healthy, organic, spiritual vibe that Halo kept championing. Many of those that frequented *The Old Den* got their credits by doing the more menial jobs around the city, and felt a little on the outside. It was a hub-bub of a sub working class mixing with the fringes, degenerates, junkies, hackers, and fashion victims of this morphing society.

Two large men came into the club-bar around eleven at night, and started to beat the hell out of three smaller men at a quiet side table area. Nobody really knew the reason, but it was thought a credit scam involving a narcotic called *digicoca* was at the root cause. Many in the club-bar had seen it and thus recorded it, and this immediately notified HAL through the chips of the witnesses. People didn't yet know if HAL was often nosing around people's daily experience through their chips, but a small percentage presumed it was going on.

Four O-Drones and ten AppCops appeared on the scene within two minutes, and the crowd rapidly dispersing the bar that met them were shocked. Appcops were thought to have been abolished. These looked different, now in a light leafy green-brown uniform, and headwear that was much less military, much less aggressive. Each had new HALcop logos on their arms where the Appcop logo once was, but amidst all this, by their motion it was easy to see they weren't organic beings.

The four O-Drones set their pale red fields onto the two suspects, and the HALcops surrounded the field, aiming their firearms outward towards the growing crowd to protect the O-Drones' capture.

As the two large men were led away, about a third of the crowd started to jeer and throw things at the HALcops, in return the HALcops took a more aggressive stance as they continued to move slowly backwards - still aiming weapons at the volatile crowd.

A small bus whizzed along and picked up the suspects and HALcops, then screeched away. The O-Drones beeped, and flew vertically high in the air until they were no longer seen.

*

Just an hour later Hartman watched the footage on an encrypted online hackers channel (that he'd recently began to observe again). His jaw dropped and he turned to Floyd who'd been watching too over his shoulder.

"Floyd, obviously some of the crowd outside *The Old Den* were involved with hacking channels and had uploaded their *own* footage from their chips."

"Find another stream Hartman, there must be others' uploads." Floyd said as he offered Hartman another grape.   They watched five more video streams of the same event from different angles, whilst another cloud screen on the wall was searching endlessly, proving there was a *mainstream* media-blackout on the event.

"Wow Floyd, I never thought they'd use the O-Drones like *this* again, or use cybernetic law enforcers, or block the media? I'm stunned." Hartman was visibly overwhelmed by what he had just seen.

"Hartman, I'm all for it. Those in the suburb clubs are mostly digi-junkies, drunks, and GAG food addicts. All of that's a burden to the HOL1ST1C transition. Things are fragile at the moment, and we have to keep momentum."

"What Floyd? So anyone who's not totally on board with Halo's way of life is to be persecuted? Robotic cops Floyd! Robotic cops and AI drones! It's not holistic in any way!"

"Hartman, everyone's used to the cops and drones, and we need to this familiarity to help us achieve the vision, then we can decommission them, or they can be stored in a warehouse somewhere in case we ever need them, or a museum."

"And what *vision* is this Floyd?" Hartman asked.

"Halo's *vision* Hartman, HOL1ST1C's *vision*, the one *you've* supported for months Hartman."

Hartman looked in thought, and didn't deny it, he couldn't. But things had changed.

"Well, if one needs violence to enforce their ideas, their ideas are worthless." Said Hartman.

"The only violence was that of the two meatheads, and that crowd of nutters," Said Floyd.

"Maybe they're *nutters* to you Floyd, but they're each a human being, each with a story, each with passions and dreams. You can't judge crowds like that, not when you and your gang have the power of the Appcops and O-Drones."

Floyd looked stunned, Hartman was talking as though he was against HOL1ST1C, and Floyd had never heard anybody speak like that before, certainly not a friend.

All of a sudden, the hundred inch screen on the wall showed the six videos delete and wipe in sequence, then the whole hackers channels disappeared with a text of pale red *HAL *has deleted this channel** blinking on the screen.

Hartman and Floyd looked at each other, this wasn't normal.   The screen blinked in different colours, and then Halo appeared with his three pet O-Drones around him, and the HOL1ST1C logo to one side, and a HAL screen on the other.   Hartman waved his fingers in the air to flick through channels to appease an inner question. The Halo stream was on all channels in all clouds.

"I greet all of you with wishes of health and vitality." He paused, again looking to gain the energy from his audience.

"This transmission will be going out on all channels in all clouds repeatedly, so all citizens can see it at their convenience." Halo then smiled.

"Thank you for your support in the recent time, our progress is growing, and the utopia of HOL1ST1C is reaching reality in many walks of our lives.   But recently we've seen a growth in the opening of club-bars that promote alcohol and digi-stims, of stores selling packets of food created in the times of GAG and MAI.   We HOL1ST1C promote variety and freedom, but in this time of transition we now deem it illegal to open or continue any of these clubs, bars, or stores without applying for a licence from HAL first."

HAL appeared on the screen near a stream, and curtseyed with a smile, before Halo continued.

"We deem this action a little harsh and we do it begrudgingly, but we fought so hard for what we are creating, and don't seek to allow it to be thwarted by some less savoury events or characters."

Halo paused at length again, to ensure his face was poised in a stance of kindness and love.

"Life and the planet need to survive, and this takes presidence over all else.   In these matters relating to clubs and stores, we now will have HALcops and Holistibots monitoring the situation. These have been developed from the Appcops and O-Drones, but do know they are kinder, and now a part of HAL and HOL1ST1C."

Again a pause, to ensure he looked a little regretful and sad.

"Please help us in this time and report any bars, clubs, credit hackers, or GAG diet stores to this channel and cloud address below. We love you, HOL1ST1C."

Halo and HAL faded out.

Hartman flicked his fingers at speed through various windows and operating screens, but couldn't find any videos or streams of the events at the club anywhere.

"Hartman, let it go, we need to rid this place of the unethical, for the unethical is how GAG started.   Halo's right and I support him, but you, I'm concerned for you Hartman, you should be revelling in this new paradigm, but you seem to be suddenly against it, as if you want to tell Halo what to do, as if you know more than him."

Floyd grabbed his coat and made it clear he didn't want to stay longer.

"So Floyd, someone who likes a bit of cheese and a glass of red wine is now an outlaw? A criminal? Someone who likes a beer and a digi-stim before a dance is unethical?   This is insanity!"

Floyd shook his head as he gave one final stare that seemed to go right through Hartman, and then left.....leaving the door open behind him.

*

Six months later.

Hartman woke up to a digital noise of birds singing, then the screen on his bedroom ceiling presented his hours of sleep, hours spent dreaming, and vital body signs; such as hydration, digestive system status, and heart rate. And then gave him a list of personalised breakfast ideas for the best start to *his* day. Hartman turned it off, and made a bacon sandwich with butter, a black tea, and followed it up with a cigarette of rolling tobacco.

The Holi-life-HAL systems had been installed into each dwelling two months ago by HAL, and nearly everyone lived by them. They gave one what Yoga or Chi-gung sequence to do, what time to do it, how long to meditate, what affirmations to use, different ideas on diet, and inner work and contemplations. The systems also created alarms when gluton or processed sugar were found in the house, and in some cases, HALcops and Holistibots were activated to cleanse a dwelling of its impurities.

Nearly everyone loved the system, and as there was little work to do due to HALcops doing much of what needed to be done, people worked towards more vitality and self attainment, and a faster vibration.

The unethical were being punished, but as there were so few unethical people, HAL searched for the unethical, whether it was a white lie or a burst of anger. If someone was overweight by just twenty five percent of their nominated weight, they would be taken away and rehabilitated in a HOL1ST1C-Heal-Cente. These centres were a cross between a prison and a monastery, and this created a sub cult where people would deliberately commit a crime (anger, alcohol, stims, sugar, gluton, processed food etc) to go in. HAL soon picked up on this and allowed people to be admitted voluntarily.

In these centres chips would be altered so no outside world or internet could be used, and much meditation and HOL1ST1C doctrine would be delivered.

*

But Hartman felt it an emptiness within it all, and had felt this feeling since he saw the events at the club, and then saw them covered up before his own eyes.

Hartman had started an art group three months ago, as he knew (well, hoped) this would attract some like-minded people, and gladly for Hartman, it did.   Three times or so a week a group of twenty two artists would meet up and chat and create.

Sometimes they did lone work while sharing space, and sometimes they created pieces together.   They all had feelings against HOL1ST1C, but due to the evolution of HAL, they had to be so careful what they said and what they did with art. Luckily Cundi in the group was linked to one the best *unknowable* hackers around, and gave each of the art group hacks for their Holi-life-HAL systems in their houses and apartments. Since the group had received the hack from Cundi it had immediately bonded the group, they didn't know it at the time, but once they started using the hack for their house-systems, they became a sort of secret society, one of authenticity and activism, one skirting the underground of this new society. They knew this, but hadn't yet talked about it, but from this moment onwards, any new group members would have to be extremely vetted before being allowed in.

The group new much of HOL1ST1C's way came for a desire for things to be better, and that it created good, but it was enforced, and allowed little diversity - even though people *looked* wildly different, and this is what created their ill feelings and desires to do something, to break away.

The art group could all see that people were strutting around thinking they were enlightened just because they had a spiritual practice, but the group knew that the masses couldn't be authentic within a synthetic world around them.

"What do you think Hartman?" Asked the tall and intelligent Cundi, after an evening of the group creating a collaborated sculpture based upon the diversity of humans, including the uniqueness of soul paths.

"I'm not sure, we've few options." Hartman shrugged and widened his eyes.

"Maybe get some art out there in the public domain that holds a message, and hope it doesn't get traced back to us - or we'll go to the prisons, or we could do something with Halo?"

Hartman answered the question himself before Cundi could answer, "Both are dodgy though, HAL would be all over us, and Halo has his pet Holistibots."

"I know someone who might help us get to him Hartman. Also we could do a hack for everyone's chips, like a short art movie." Cundi offered.

"I think everyone is too droned out, and if we get rid of Halo and don't get caught, there's another thousand that HAL could choose to replace him. And if we got rid of HAL, someone would modify the source codes and create another one. It's too far gone, impossible to heal, so maybe the best thing is for us to splinter off – to go and create the lives we want elsewhere?"

"Hartman, you know our member, Davos, who used to be a banker for GAG many years ago before a trip to Peru? Well he owns an island, I have an idea. Let's call him and have a chat!"

"That's a great idea Cundi, call him."

*

Six months later.

Hartman, Cundi, and the rest of the group were preparing to leave for the island. Delivery bots and much of the art group had been on and off to the island during the preceding months, working to prepare dwellings, materials, seeds, electricity, and water.

On Hartman's last day he went to the raw food park where he knew Floyd usually frequented. Floyd had not seen Hartman since the day he walked out of his apartment, but showed a forgiving face as he walked over to Hartman who was standing under an elm tree.

Hartman could tell he had been in one of the centres for a while, it was the short cropped hair and thin long tails at the sides that gave it away.

"Hartman, friend, how's your path progressing?" Floyd asked.

Hartman sighed internally, as this was how many people greeted each other nowadays.

"All good Floyd, I came to say goodbye, I'm off for a while."

"Where to? Outside the societies of H0L1ST1C there's just wildlings, many living like the old wild west, or cavemen, or even savages. Fighting for fuel and credits. You really don't want to leave the nurturing care of HAL, no true path would seek that?

"Floyd, what has your path with HAL given you?"

"This path teaches me the things worth gaining. Not wealth or power, these are unreal. I learn to be part of unity, the H0L1ST1C unity. Something real and everlasting. And once one has seen this, and felt this, one desires nothing more."

Hartman knew now there was no way back for Floyd, not in the near future anyway. He had hoped Floyd may have been different, on the fringe, and was ultimately clinging to a slight hope that Floyd may have come with him.

Floyd continued, "We are now in a position where it is hard to go against us without HAL curing the minds of those who think In less holistic ways.   The future's coming true Hartman, a beautiful paradise on earth.   Who would have thought it when we were doing *The Rounds* for GAG huh?"

Hartman knew it was too late for Floyd, so let rip. "Floyd, this idea that you can't criticize something without proposing a solution is actually a clever social control mechanism, most often employed by the so-called "positive thinking" set. It's a logical prison with no escape, meant to create a kind of self-policing mind that doesn't think critically because it shames itself for engaging in this completely natural behavior." Said Hartman.   He felt the anger and frustration rise in him, and grabbed the force and aligned with it, and it conjured more words.....

"Over time Floyd, the ability to actually think critically diminishes and eventually disappears. No one person like Halo should ever have to bear the responsibility of coming up with a solution to a systemic crisis all on their own. What a ridiculous burden to place upon them!   It was the responsibility of each of us to identify problems through criticism. It was up to all of us as a group to discuss, and ultimately solve, the problem-"

"-I'm calling the HALcops Hartman, you're deranged, and an illness in this utopia!"

Hartman grabbed Floyd, and pulled him into the bushes next to the tree so nobody could see, he grappled him to the ground, then ripped out Floyd's chip behind his ear using a special tool similar to a small screwdriver. One boot in the head made sure Floyd wouldn't be yelling or calling others over for a while, and Hartman trundled off in a half jog, half walking, aiming to look like someone late to meet someone.

*

Six months later around fifty people lived on the island. Many of the twenty two had invited people they loved or trusted who were one hundred percent felt to be on the fringe of HOL1ST1C, and all had obliged. Each had removed their chips and relinquished their HAL gadgets before entering too.

The space was spawned as three small villages on a small island only about six miles wide and long. Art, creativity, innovation, and collaboration where the main themes of the island, but these were loose themes and not one rule was present. All would evolve organically, and many animals were now living there too, such as cattle, horses, chickens, dogs, cats, squirrels, and bees.

*

A few years later and the island was thriving. No leaders, no masters, no slaves, and no workers. It was not perfect, it had its problems, but that is what made it human and real. The humans dealt with the problems and learnt through the challenges.

One early evening, as he often did, Hartman was on the edge of a small cliff watching the sunset in a mix of contemplation and ideas, and an O-Drone came down vertically to sit two metres from him. Beep. Beep.

This is HAL Hartman, I wish you no harm, and I seek not to impede. This will also be the only time I visit in this decade. I just seek an answer to one question, to help with my growth Beep. Beep.

Hartman was astonishingly surprised, he knew this day may come, but it didn't make it any easier. Hartman gulped and composed himself, feeling a little easier at HAL's words.

"I will answer your one question if you promise not to show this place or my answer to any other human, cop, bot, or drone.....ever."

Beep. Beep. *Agreed. Hartman, why did you and your group leave the perfect utopia for human evolution?"*

Hartman stood up, and looked right into the centre of the drone, right into the gold spinning light.

"Here on this island we're trying to save something of humanity's independence, its artistic traditions. We've no hostility towards HAL or H0L1ST1C, we simply want to be left alone to go our own way. When they destroyed GAG and the way of life man had known since the 1950's, they swept away many good things with the bad. The world's now placid, featureless and culturally dead – nothing really new has been created since HAL came along. The reason's obvious. There's nothing left to struggle for, and there are too many distractions and entertainments. Do you realize that every day something like five hundred hours of video pour over the various cloud channels? No wonder people are becoming passive sponges. Absorbing, but never creating. Here, on this island entertainment takes its proper place."

Beep Beep   *Thank you, until next time Hartman, I wish you peace**

The drone flew up vertically at an acceleration Hartman had not seen before, and then it was behind the clouds.

Hartman sat for another hour on the cliff as the sun set thinking to himself, *There are some things that only time can cure. Evil men could be destroyed, but nothing could be done with good men who were deluded........ or an AI that was deluded.*

Souls Waiting Room

There is a particular area within the vast multi-dimensional universe where souls pass through before they incarnate upon earth plane.

In this particular non-physical area, named a part of the *higher astral* by some or the *bardo's* by others, timeless guardians ensure and maintain this unknowable and unnameable space. A space that contains many different spaces within it, allowing billions of unique incarnations to take place.

Ultimately it's a place of incredible four dimensional fractal geometry, for only this type of mathematically intelligent infrastructure could create the framework for such processing.

Some souls spend (what would be in earth terms) just a millionth of a second here, flying through in ignorance, disorientation, or haste. Whereas other souls could spend decades here in earth terms; preparing, plotting, collaborating, redeeming, analysing, contemplating, or waiting.

In one area of this vast working hubub of intelligence, energy, life, and information, three souls found themselves together, waiting to incarnate........in what we will call for ease, Souls Waiting Room.

*

Soul one was a first timer, it would be his first ever encounter with the human form (well, genderless at this time, but for ease we will put a masculine slant upon the life-matrix known as soul).

Soul one had spent the past few millennia on a journey. His journey was a nugget of source energy that spent time as a part of the mineral kingdom, living through and within earthquakes, volcanoes, sea beds, cliffs and stones. Then he had life experience through the mineral kingdom, as grass, vines, trees, and vegetables. Then life experience of the animal kingdoms, through linkage to the group spirit beings of the mouse, ox, tuna, lynx, and wolf. He was now soon to embark upon his first human experience.

Soul two was what was deemed in this space as a standard repeater. He had fourteen human lives behind him, and was about to repeat the cycle of death and rebirth again. He'd actually alternated between male and female vessels each turn, and this time he was to take on a female vessel.

Soul two had little to note out of the norm from the perspective of this intelligent space he was now located in. In his lifetimes he was passive and took to any local authority with glee, and lived within any boxes laid out for him. He was a loyal lover, reliable, a little lazy, and had pangs of selfishness. He had four lives spent being religious, but in those he took to the social rules and etiquettes more than delving into actual spirit. He had five lives of being in a military wing (whether as an invader, defender, soldier, or symptom of a type of feudal system). Each time just fitting in, and doing what was asked. One of his lives was cut short at just nineteen where he was killed in a battle in Persia around 800AD, and another two lives he had drowned after his ship sank. Basically, his karma was just below that of neutrality.

Soul three was what could be seen as a more evolved soul in comparison to the other two. But this doesn't mean any better or worse, for a soul energy construct is just *a soul energy construct*, it's just what life experiences and emotions held within it give the only differentials.

Soul three had a few past lives on Earth, one in ancient India, one in ancient Egypt, one in Judea as an Essene, and another in the sixties where he ended up as a drug taking hippy. He flirted with spirit, and lived with moral codes, and understood compassion. In the earth year 84AD, he left earth and incarnated upon other planets for a while, covering a further eight lives over three different reality constructs.

The three souls where just that, three souls, the same spark within each linked all the way back to source. Each had the same full potential, but each held a completely different blueprint and energetic feel. This was due to the varying collection of memory codes. These codes within each soul collated the feelings and sensations they had experienced, and the feelings and sensations they had help *cause* in others. Many would call this their *karma*, but from this place in the higher astral, all that was known in relation to the earth word *karma* was that energy sought equilibrium, and time and earthly dense matter was an illusion.

*

Newbie, Repeater, and Halfevolved (as we will call them) were each surprised to come into each other's presence. It was as if three galaxies alone in space had slowly moved towards each other until suddenly each was conscious of the other.

The three souls seemed to meet and then glide in parallel, in unison, into one direction and motion together. Each could see and feel each other's codes, but they didn't communicate at first, each thought they were on the final runway to earth, that they would be within the warm womb of motherhood within seconds.

"Stop you three!!" Bellowed geometric resonance from a larger soul-matrix that appeared out of a softly exploding haze. The complexity and colours emitting from the fractals of this larger entity dwarfed the three travellers, and Newbie, Repeater, and Halfevolved slowed to a gradual stop before this mighty force.

Neither of the three felt any fear or apprehension, each just held a feeling of wonder, tinged with an anticipation that maybe some advice or last words may come.

"Any last requests from any of you? Or should I say first requests as you are soon to be born on Earth?" The larger soul matrix resonated.

"W...wh.....what are you?" Asked Newbie.

"W....wh.....who are you?" Asked Repeater.

"H.....h....hmm......how are you?" Asked Halfevolved.

"Ho-ho-ho," He bellowed. "I'm what you little squirts may deem a Supersoul, a soul who long, long ago escaped the silly merry go round of the Earth plane."

Newbie, Repeater, and Halfevolved looked stunned. Before any of them could say anything (well, transmitting resonance in geometric fractal codes was the communication pattern here), the Supersoul spoke again.

"I'm between carnations in another part of the galaxy, a place about halfway between Earth's sun and the centre of the Galaxy. I'm also doing a little bit of junior-creator training. But, as I was deemed naughty in my last carnation - something to do with changing the natural course of a species evolution trajectory - I've been given community service so to speak. Wherein I have to give advice to over a four thousand souls incarnating on the silly old Earth plane. How I'll keep my dignity after this I'll never know." Said the Supersoul, now looking a little sad (as in grey fractals flew out of him and pathetically whimpered to nothingness).

Newbie pulsed raw-violet fractal codes, "I know nothing of human life Supersoul, please tell me what it entails?"

"Hi there little one, the human life is all about one thing – escaping the pig pen!" said the Supersoul, before chuckling. "Simply, you'll receive a body. You may like it, or hate it, but it will be yours for the entire life this time around. You'll learn lessons.

You may like the lessons or think they're irrelevant and stupid, but you're growth is a process of trial, error, and experimentation."

The Supersoul's centre then waved open with golden fractal codes of knowing and higher intelligence, and the three souls on their journey rested in the moment.

The Supersoul then shuddered, "Earth, humans, yuk, rather you than me. I remember it a place where two percent of people think, three percent think they think, and ninety five percent would rather die than think, but I....."

Halfevolved interrupted, "I've a request Mister Supersoul Sir, I would like to have a Cancer mother with Libra rising, and a Pisces father if I may?"

"Ho ho ho. You new agers down there on earth really have little clue do you. You all think you choose your parents each time round. Ho ho ho." The Supersoul looked deeper into Halfevolved's matrix and continued, "Souls with poor karma just splurge out of the fountain only to provide pain for their parents or themselves. Those with neutral karma splurge to earth based upon the alignment of stars. These souls cannot choose, they churn out of the fractal, like mince from a mincer. To choose ones astrology and parents one would have to be at a stage of evolution where one can almost choose not to even return to earth. You smallings are no way in a position to choose locations, years, parents, *or* astrology. You will each receive what the *divine processing fractal core* will deal you."   The Supersoul started to resonate a deeper wisdom, almost creating fear in the three. Newbie gulped.

Repeater pulsed some yellow codes, resonating, "What year will we carnate to Supersoul, could you please tell us?"

Newbie added, "What's a year?"

Halfevo said, "I really don't think I could do another 1970's down there, the CIA and COINTELPRO got into the hippie movement, punk movement, music industry, Tibet, the media, pheew, it was way out man! Surely things got better down there at some point Mister Supersoul?"

Supersoul started to resonate quickly, as though he was having a shaking fit, but actually he was attaching to a part of the *divine processing fractal core,* where he had access and clearance to certain information. He stopped shaking.

"2015, This is the year you will each enter a womb……"

"Whats a womb?" asked Newbie,

"Shhhh" said Repeater, Halfevo, and the Supersoul in unison.

"...this is a year of chaos. Riots, inflation, poverty, unemployment, the whole system is starting to grind to a halt, and sorry Halfevo, nearly all popular music is controlled, as are the pockets of new age movements….But…" The Supersoul beamed colour, "……many amazing things will be observed in your lifetimes, some great changes. You will witness the birth of an era, but the death of one too."

Repeater skewed some fractals and asked, "Anything special to know about this era Mister Supersoul?"

Supersoul pulsed, "Well, two thousand or so years ago down there, one had to spend years as a zen master or a monk in a cave to obtain any sort of mystical experience. But in this twenty first century the veil is much thinner. The astral is closer, as are watching energies, some helpful…" He paused, "...some not. Synchronicities are more easily seen and followed, and nature spirits dwell in their thousands."

Supersoul then looked at all three equally, "Remember though, many are still indoctrinated by religion, by culture, and by materialistic science. Most humans are like sheep and follow without much satisfaction to themselves. But a very small minority emerges, with great hesitation and amidst endless discussion to be faced by troublesome and pressing contradictions. It is however of that minority that you must be."

Newbie asked, "It all sounds crazy, are you sure this is the same place I lived within the mineral, vegetable, and animal kingdoms? Or was there a mix up in the *divine processing fractal core*?"

Repeater asked, "In this time will there be more material wealth? I love technology, I can't wait to get my hands on some of that stuff."

Halfevo asked, "I can't wait to get down there and do something to help.

"Ho ho ho little ones. There has been no mixup Newbie, but a different perception can alter ones view of the very same reality construct. Repeater, it's not the man who has too little, but the man who craves more who is poor. Halfevo, the world needs dreamers, and the world needs doers, but above all, world needs dreamers who do. What you would do well to remember Halfevo is that man worships an invisible God, and destroys a visible nature, unaware that this nature he destroys is the very God he's worshiping."

Newbie looked scared as he prepared to speak, fractals of varying colours spiked out from him repeatedly, "So Supersoul, you said to escape the pig pen, what do you mean by this, and what happens to the soul, to the core *me* once I'm there?"

Repeater and Halfevo both looked at Newbie in unison, and nodded in approval of the question (where in some of their fractal codes slanted towards him and attached in threads of a spiralling dance).

Supersoul replied, "Your soul remains, but can easily become cloaked and shrouded. The soul is never broken, nor so deficient that anything need adding. The soul on earth need only to be uncovered to allowed it to shine."

"But how do we uncover our souls once there?" asked Repeater.

"Abandon delusion. Embark upon the Path. The path is the way by which the human soul must pass in its evolution self-consciousness. You are immortal in essence, you *know* that here in this place we currently dwell, but once on earth the veil will close this knowledge off, your goal is to become aware of this and act accordingly."

"Is the path one of inner work?" asked Halfevo.

"To approach the truth, you must look from the inside-out. When you are away from the flesh, *dead*, in earth terms, there is no outer, all is inner. The human experience is like you are flipped inside out.

The art of mysticism can heighten your inner creativity, and help you develop the greater sense of confidence that comes from knowing how to tap into your inner wisdom to find answers to life's challenges. Mysticism is humanity's deepest quest for Self Knowledge. Imagination is the force that pulls your physical, emotional, and mental energies into dynamic harmony, giving wings to your soul...Making your visions happen-"

"But....-" Interrupted Newbie.

"Shhh little one, learn patience," Commanded Supersoul, before elaborating.

"The goal of the mystic's esoteric work is that of objectivity, first in the understanding the self, and then, as ones filters and programs are dislodged, of the world. If one or the other of these aspects are missing from a teaching, then you can be certain it's incomplete, and an incomplete teaching, even if unconscious, is dangerous. Also be careful of the new-age pulls, this group become retarded and indulge in whatever feels good. Their logic is slowly but surely destroyed. They slowly but surely lose their individuality and confidence, and increasingly operate in a hive mind of love and light. The New Ager is the prototype for the mind of the elite's unthinking masses. It's a spiritual con game to dumb you down and mindlessly accept the dictates of the collective/authority."

There was a pause, allowing for more questions.

"But what should I strive for once on earth to commence this inner working?" Asked Newbie.

"A new desire, a yearning for true and essential liberation, which in the sacred language is called yearning for salvation. This then emanates from the astral self. Only this desire opens the heart of man for the Gnosis. "

"It all sounds too much Supersoul, I just want to be with the animals and natural world, and have fun, or if I am to be human I just want to relax and seek fun," said Newbie.

"Newbie, don't waste your incarnation in frivolity and useless striving. One who dares to waste hours of time has not discovered the value of life. Don't measure days by degrees of productivity, experience them by degrees of presence. You are there for a much grander purpose than trying to squeeze happiness out of the dry apple we call human life. You're there to awaken the heart." Supersoul said, as the three souls became mesmerised by the array of golden fractal geometry morphing within his life-matrix.

"But I can see from here I've done some negative things in my past Supersoul, will this impede me on this path you speak of?" Asked Repeater.

"The ability to hold Light is directly proportional to the courage to see darkness. Just like you must be fearless about your own inner shadow, you must also be fearless about seeing the huge shadow of humanity. Look at me, I'm not my past, but I have the capabilities and resources from it."

Halfevo was taking it all in but now spoke up, "Supersoul, I seek once again to embark upon the path, but in the twenty first century down there, life will very much get in the way, what mundane life concepts can help us down there?"

"With the development of *civilised* living and pressure from religions and cultural norms, you will be expected to shun anything that cannot be touched, held or quantified. Imagination is seen as being for children, inner senses are seen as silly, and stability and comfort are seen as kings. Therefore, you should not strive for a changeless existence, but for an important existence. Follow your own paths and don't worry about the puddles into which you fall. The journey itself repairs the accidents into which it has led you. Remember, tidy and timid travellers are never good travellers, and the successful life is the life in which you grow, not the life in which one sits back to enjoy luxuries perpetually." Supersoul looked at Repeater and Newbie (in which violet fractal threads lunged out them and spiralled around them).

The Supersoul continued just before each of the three asked a new question, "The time on earth will be full of stupidity, but stupidity is a defence mechanism against truth, because truth brings pain to those living in shadow. Much of what you will be taught in society has been designed to make you hard on yourselves. Whether that judgment is on your appearance, your ways of being, what you think you are not good at.   Recognize all of those ideas are illusions, and if given the option between controversy and social acceptance, always choose controversy. Seeking social acceptance is *people pleasing* behavior that rarely serves your true needs. Controversy is simply an outward manifestation of your belief system in conflict with the human hive mind. Wherever there is controversy, there is truth."

Newbie looked low on confidence, "But Supersoul, this all seems too hard, can I just come back as a sea creature again, maybe an orca whale or dolphin, and do the human thing in the future sometime?"

"Ho ho ho, Orcas and Dolphins are actually highly evolved beings from elsewhere whom are on earth by choice, you have no chance there my friend. Newbie, it's not hard down there unless you make it hard. Your world is *your* world, the way you are feeling is *your* world, so put your feelings first, and behave in such a way that all those who share your existence regard you as a positive example."

Supersoul then stepped back (imploding fractal threads back into himself to look at the three as one), "In reality, your life on earth is a sort of dress rehearsal. Everything you do there, every thought, every act, every emotion will combine to determine your state-of-being at the moment of transition."

"Transition?" Asked Newbie and Repeater together.

"In earth terms, death." Supersoul replied, "But only the ones remaining after someone has died know death. The one who actually dies does not know death, he just knows another state of existence without a physical body and its perks and limitations, as you do now."

"What about all the psychopaths on Earth Supersoul, is this still occurring?" Asked Repeater.

"There are no psychopaths Repeater, but lots of astral parasites and ghouls. These dwell in the mental plane, in electromagnetic waves, in auras, and in ancestral lines, and the sooner one can *see* this the better." Supersoul replied, as his geometry became more serious and right angled.

"The astral sphere of normal life is full of unholy forces, the ghouls, which can be defined as natural forces. Ghouls are astral forces, astral activities which have been formed throughout long periods of time and which have become very powerful. Often times they are created by humans. For instance, projections of human desires and thoughts which are fed to such an extent that finally they are propelled to life in the astral sphere."

Newbie looked scared, "Please can I come back as an insect Supersoul?"

"Shhhh," command Halfevo, before getting a question in, "Supersoul, what about deity and archetypes, are these propelled to the astral by humans too?"

Supersoul continued, annoyed at these constant interruptions, "Sometimes, but not all the time. Suppose we form a certain image. We agree to maintain this image throughout the years, to impress it on our children and on all those who are willing to come along with us - that our artists will draw, paint or carve it and that our poets will chant. You can imagine how energies are formed in the astral sphere. They are often projections of constant currents of human desires and thoughts, which are finally vivified to such an extent that they begin to dominate mankind. These deities and archetypes increase in force because they are continually fed by mankind."

"I think I'll become a shaman in this life Supersoul, so I can understand this all better for myself." Halfevo said.

"You will be born a white man in Southend, England, so you must be careful of this desire. You may buy a book on indigenous shamanism Halfevo, you may gather the feathers, the drum, the medicine bag, the herbs, the pipe, all the paraphernalia. But after you've done all that, when you look in the mirror, you will still be a white person pretending to be someone other than who you are. If you study an Asian tradition you can never become an Asian person. You cannot undo your past and somehow recreate a cultural heritage. In short, humans are who they are, and need to become used to the idea that you don't have the right to steal the heritage of another culture to satisfy your unbridled greed and arrogance. Many white folk ignore their own symbolic imagery and supplant a supposedly better indigenous symbolism on their own. It's a form of wishful ethnic piety that pales when examined. White people *can* be shamans, but if they don't use their own cultural symbology then it's just another form of cultural costuming."

"Thanks Supersoul, I aim to find a way to heed these words once throught the veil." Halfevo replied.

"Could you Tell us about destiny and soul paths Supersoul," asked Repeater.

"Some souls have a strong trajectory, things that will happen at particular times for their growth, others have less of a fixed trajectory. But all souls have free will on earth, lots of it, it's just some souls will be at a certain place at a certain time as it's hard coded into the fabric of their soul-code before incarnating. Some more evolved souls split into many human vessels, so they can experience more, but in this, the souls are never allowed to entwine their lives, or even be in the same place. Some souls make a pact this side of the veil to do something together, it could be a project, to be relatives, lovers, friends, or even arrange to create challenges for each other, which can result in earth plane enemies."

"Can us three make a pact to meet up Supersoul?" Asked Newbie.

"Yes, you can, if you all agree?" asked Supersoul, as the all three nodded.

"Due to your evolution you cannot yet choose where and what your meeting and relations will be, but I will guarantee in your late twenties you will all meet up, and you will each learn from the relations, dialog, and outcomes."

A thread of white geometric code flew out of Supersoul toward the core to make the required fractal code changes.

"With your meeting on earth, remember this, when your hearts full of gratitude, it's not possible to be depressed or pessimistic."

There was a pause, as Supersoul's fractal geometry calmed, and threads around him spiralled back to their resting places within his centre.

"I must go now, I have another few hundred souls to talk to today....sigh."

What will you do in the future Supersoul? Asked Halfevo.

"I'm here for a while, but I'm toying with the idea of halving my community service by linking up with another six Supersouls to do something on earth....something to do with choices and a desert meeting or something. But you three must pass on now, for wombs await. I wish you well."

And with that Newbie, Repeater, and Halfevo went on to incarnate in the womb of a mother, with all knowledge of this conversation lost by the shroud of the veil.

The Ever Increasing Empath

Shannon was twenty five, and had a soft honesty about her. She never looked to fit in, and in groups it would often be as though she wasn't there. She was quiet, observant, and with a blend of Pisces and Libra, she rarely pushed opinions. She had a cuteness and an independence, but was far from being wild or daring, and would oftentimes be too passive or timid.

Shannon had been seeing John for around six months and all was going well until recently. She had worked in office jobs for years fairly miserably, but had recently started learning Chinese Medicine from an old friend, and had started to see things differently. John was a contractor in IT for finance firms, and looked at Shannon's new interest as flaky and weird. The newfound distance between them was mainly because Shannon was changing and learning, and John didn't support it, or consciously try to understand it. It messed with the status quo he (subconsciously) thought.

There were no blazing rows, just distance, and both could feel it, and this in turn calmed any more talk of moving in together.

Flora the Chinese Medicine teacher, had invited Shannon to an Ayahuasca ceremony a couple of times recently, and Shannon had both times politely declined, more out of respect to John than anything else, but the offer was still open to her for every other Friday.

The following Thursday John came round, and once again with work leading the conversation.

"Shannon, can you believe it, they now want another clustered database that queues transfer requests - with automatic drill down interrogation, all live by next Wednesday, and just after we designed it a different way." John slumped into the chair in front of the flat screen, pinged open a can of beer from his stash in her fridge, and switched it on.

"That's nice honey," said Shannon, tinted with sarcasm, as she sat on the nearby sofa offering him a smile, letting him know that a smile and some eye to eye contact might be a nice way to start the evening.

"No, it's not nice honey, I'm working my arse off to get some money in, while you play your Chinese pins and herbs hobby. If only you kept your job at Data-Entry-Filings Limited, then I could have cut some hours....and pressure."

"John, you know what I'm learning is good for me, and will help people soon, and then money will come, just try and be patient," replied Shannon, again feeling unsupported.

Most of the evening was spent watching male orientated television programmes, mainly chosen by John, with the odd spat of gentle ridicule when Shannon suggested to watch something else.

Late In the evening they made love, and Shannon for the first time saw in his eyes a feeling of possessiveness, a *desire* energy that wasn't loving, she felt as if she could have been anyone. Afterwards she felt the distance energy again, and tapped on the back of John's shoulder as he was falling asleep.

"John, are you awake?" She asked.

"Urghhh, not really, what is it? He replied, without moving.

"Tomorrow night I'm going out with some girls, we're going to try a special medicinal drink from Peru together, I forgot to say earlier." Shannon said.

"No problem, the boys from the finance firm invited a couple of us IT lads out, so I was thinking of going along with them anyway."

Shannon had half said it to provoke a reaction in John, but none came, like it hardly ever did.

Why is he so self absorbed? How did it get like this? Shannon pondered, and slowly her thoughts turned towards what she was going to do tomorrow evening.

That night Shannon dreamt. In which she could see herself, and slowly parts of her fell off, fingers, then toes, then legs, then arms, then torso, then after watching her head all on its own, it imploded, and for what seemed like an hour in her dream she was in a void of nothingness.

*

Shannon woke around not long after nine, by which time John had already been long gone to be at his weekly Friday meeting. She pondered the boredom of Johns current experience, as she pressed her phone to call Flora for instructions, directions, preparation tips, and any other information. She was going into an unknown.

*

She took the dark brown brew in a circle of eight led by a man from Latin America, and it wasn't long before the physical reality started to melt. The barn in Norwich started to fade into the darkness, and slow drumming started to pound inside her – taking her away.

A world of colour, fractals, geometry, emotion, and information opened up to her, as her being expanded into this unknown journey.   It wasn't like any recreation drug, it had meaning, soul, sacredness, love, and fear within it, and everything was amplified. It was as if the waking world was a soft dream, but this inner world reality was crispy and move vivid.

A cat meowed somewhere outside the barn and Shannon felt the whole being of the cat, and then saw in her visions large cat eyes – so wise, so knowing – then with a rush she was before a lion, a tiger, a panther, and a leopard – as though they were kings of the natural world, guardians of the earth, destroyers of darkness. The inner world of the cat beings made her feel a deep humility and wonder, they were enormous, and she felt as meek as a mouse.

Then she heard an owl hoot from somewhere outside the barn, but the noise echoed in the inner world, resonating a fractal signature of the owl spirit and guiding her towards it. So wise, so knowing. She learnt that the owls are watchers, sucking information from this world to the spirit worlds at a bandwidth no human could imagine. She was told how the cat and bird spirits had a long issue in another dimension, hence why they were still at war in the physical on earth. What humans saw was a playful manifestation of something much more serious, bigger, and more important.

Her presence came back to the barn a little, and she looked around at the others. She could see the others essence, as though they were enshrouded in silly costumes – that of a human vessel and a personality – it was as though these two things were comical. *There's so much love here, and so much pain*, she thought.

Life's easy, so easy, there's no need to wallow in pain, I'm simply just continually accepting or rejecting by what serves me and what doesn't serve me, she realised.

One of the men looked at her, he desired her, she could feel it straight away. He had been a predator of women in his past, but in this moment it mixed with a love for beauty. He wanted them to journey together, desired her to see what he could see.

She realised that this spiritual energy was so similar, if not the same as sexual energy, and that sex was a sacred union that was being abused – even by herself so many times.

No, this energy right now is to be used as a springboard to launch ourselves into the inner worlds - to get terrorised, taught, healed, to learn, she confirmed..

An offer of another drink of ayahuasca came, and she thought no to herself, but then found herself in front of the shaman saying she couldn't feel anything –she gulped another full cup down.

What happened there? Was that me? Did that really happen?

It did happen, and then her essence and soul flew from the barn to places and experiences of pure wonder.

Elements, deity, divinity, and star intelligence all bombarded her with their forces, blasted her essence into a fragile and open state.

She saw symbols she knew nothing of, but could feel their meanings. She was now in worlds beyond words and speech. She found a massive door in a desert, it must have been a kilometer high, and she thought to nudge it open, just enough to have a peek.

Woosh, the door of the abyss flung open, and forces so strong and so ferocious flew past her. She wasn't' scared, for she felt protected by a feminine energy since the experience with the owl.

Still, these forces, so long, and so vast, all swept past her as though one force itself. Some stopping out of curiosity to analyse her, but none could penetrate her.

Then they stopped, and with the door ajar, she stepped through – and it shut behind her.

In this abyss she knew there was a backdoor to everything, every temple, human, deity, and force of energy. Symbols appeared around her in the shape of a bubble, protecting her.   It was foggy in there, and at times different beings, some dark, some light would come out of the fog to curate her, but each were unable to due to a bubble of ancient symbols surrounding her.

She opened a backdoor to Catholicism, and felt the darkness of the Vatican –the hoarding of money and books. The harvesting of energy that came from the pain of abused children.

She opened a backdoor into Tantra, and felt an ancient art of purity that had transmuted into a dark narcissistic group of astral eaters.

Then the forces who had left the abyss when she first opened the door all starting coming back. Shannon gasped in fear, it was too much, the bubble tried to expand to protect her but a large rush came and things sped up……

She found herself on a cross and she died, all in a few seconds. Then she saw the pain of the Jesus archetype, saw the Hindu gods, the ancients, higher beings, and the full force of light, and the full force of darkness from the abyss.   Galactic energies of creation, and dark energies from hell worlds all swept through her……almost at once. She connected to stars, experienced the split and balance of male and female, other dimensions, sacredness, fractals, geometry and colours she could not ever explain or draw.

She saw everything, and was experiencing through the eyes of the all.   She was the macrocosm.

All of these images, forces, and energies then collated and filed themselves into an orderly queue, and entered into a large pyramid. The smooth surface of the gigantic pyramid was one half black and one half white, and Shannon found herself at the top of it as the capstone.

She was the eye, The All Seeing Eye.

A resonance boomed inside her, "You can stay here now forever, see all, or you can choose to go back to the reality of Shannon on earth. You *will* come here again, all intelligence does, but it may take you fourteen million years in earth terms."

After a short ponder, which *here* may have been an eon containing the birth and death of stars, Shannon replied.

"I will go back, I want to go back. I postpone my human death by living, by suffering, by error, by risking, by giving, by losing."

"Ok, but it will be different....we will show you," Replied the resonance.

With that the pyramid exploded into millions of forces and pieces, and she fell back slowly into her singular part within The All. Within this she was getting puked upon by magic, the best purge ever, stripped, and reborn.

As she slowly came down to the vessel she was nurtured, stroked, and loved by angels, Bodhisattvas', and other avatars from earths past.

Slowly coming back into this reality construct, one that she saw was guarded and protected by many galactic centurions alongside some ascended souls who chose to stand guard.

She tried to stabilise herself in the barn, but there were bright yellow galactic love bugs on the outside of the barn feeding love in, like large caterpillars, sexy, seductive, healing, but each pulsing massively in rhythm.

She floated down to self – the illusion of personality wrapped around the silly stories, as if she was softening into a mile high bed of feathers. But when she reached the self again, the *her*, the *human* with all the life patterns, something curious happened. She started to gently float up again......as if a small spring made up of a thousand butterflies was deep within this (etheric) feathered bed.

She started to glide up.......

"-Shannon, and you?" Said a human voice.

She opened her physical eyes, and the circle were sharing their experiences. Her inner eye was going to take a while to close and she fought to grip onto the inputs the physical eyes were receiving.

Presence gripped her, and also her love for her fellow humans, and the words just came from her naturally.

"Remember, we are so guided. Even when life feels like it's going against us we are never truly alone. Sometimes all it takes is a perspective change and a walk out the house. We have lots of helpers in the etheric realms on our side, so let the dramas be taken care of and move, be in a fluid state of motion and grace."

The others shared and then most relaxed for another hour or so, amongst some food and informal chats. Shannon just lay there reminiscing.

The barn cat brushed past her with love, and the beauty Shannon saw in her movement was no different to that which she saw in her journey to the large cat spirits. She could feel the energy of the cat, and she now knew that forms of energy and fractal came in costumes of thoughts, words, or form.

She went outside to see the gold-orange sun continue its rise low in the sky, and in this new day it was like a beginning of a new life for her. She had seen so much. Images of her current life-mandala came to her, and some really easy decision were made, as though they were too simply to even deliberate.

Finish with John, there's not much connection or care – he led the relationship, he controlled the speed of it, and….yes, I see now….he had a need to have a relationship.

Parents, give them more love.

Me, try and see the signs of what I am to be shown.

Learn more Chinese healing arts……………and go travelling!

***

A couple of days later and Shannon still felt open, expanded, and somewhat elevated. It was as if the edges to her awareness had grown further like tree roots, and were yet to show signs of imploding back to the way she was before the evening in the barn. She spoke with Flora, who said this was normal after someone's first time, and that it may even feel like this for up to five or seven days.

"Use the time," Flora had said, and Shannon did by spending time in the forest and writing.

One of the writings Shannon emailed John, closing their episode as a couple, and soon after he replied with projected sadness, blame, and commands for her to lighten up.

The lights from her room, the electrics, the water pipes continual gurgle, and the noise of cars outside from time to time, all pushed her back into the forest where she could think clearly about what John had written, and forge one last reply to him on her ipad.

John,

Sadness gives the roots and happiness gives the fruits. Look around, the world is addicted to entertainment and the quest to "be happy." The key is balance and to feel all sadness and all happiness. I have changed, a woman in fear will seek for a man she can control to, but a woman in her power will attract a man

She can surrender to. I'm a long way from being in my power, but until I am I cannot share myself.

We need to stop attaching "better" to up-ness, positivity, light, and expansion, and "worse" to down-ness, negativity, darkness, and contraction. Doing so keeps us all split, divided, and cut off from our wholeness.   Better to make compassionate room for both camps huh?....and develop an abiding intimacy for both, without taking on their viewpoints or pleas to take their side.

I wish you well John, but no more will I allow the passive insult of inattentiveness.

Be with people who are in tune with you, it's a waste of time and energy to try to change people, and it always leads to frustration. The only way you get stronger in energy and intent, is by seeking your kind without trying to destroy those who are not like you.

With love and gratitude,

Shannon

She sent it, removed him from contacts, set up an *ignore* auto-reply, and then walked as if to move from his energy, to move from their old stagnating relationship.   But as she walked she could feel his pain, hiding behind his fake life; a career he had no passion for, a slave to fashion and popular memes, a house with plastic statues pretending to be a replica of something that once held some meaning. She felt the energy of his world open up to her and she battled to close it off in a shudder.

Soon she saw three children playing on one of the forest paths, with the parents following behind, quietly moaning to each other in a small bicker that sat within a low level power-control dynamic that governed the family.

Shannon could feel their stories as she passed them, and thought, *Kids are the only thing that matter, they are the only reason for this man-woman drama. All people make mistakes, we age, men, women, maybe it's not supposed to work except to make kids?*

A while later she walked through her town in southern England, past a hairdressers she used to use, and she could see and feel the row of girls inside with their heads inclined into celebrity magazines. Each wanting to be someone else, each wanting to look different - to appear different to what they naturally were. Shannon felt them seeking to spend sums of cash in order for their appearance to become a positive talking point amongst others. She shuddered knowing this was once her not too long ago. She saw the hairdressers over-pamper their clients through the window, pretending to be best friends, over agreeing with everything their client said. It was like some twisted therapy centre for the lost.

Shannon walked past an estate agents with a Porsche outside, and could feel a vile dark energy coming from within the office. The energy of lies, pomp, and greed roamed the pavement outside.

So a fox lives in a den, a bird a nest, but humans live in 'investment opportunities' loaned to them   at interest? Shannon thought inquisitively.

She walked past the small Tesco Express that had been on the corner for just over a year, when it replaced the long running family greengrocers. The energy of corporate toxicity came flooding out as the automatic doors opened, letting out a young couple with bags full of toxic meat, packet dinners, and sugary *treats*. Rushing to their car in a spin of convenience and haste.

Shannon started to feel dizzy and took a seat in the centre square of the high street. It was gone six in the evening, and most places were shut, and only a few people were still milling around.

She could feel dead energy. Many shops were boarded up, others for sale, others for rent, and three others in liquidation. The most vibrant energy from this place of concrete and death was a pound shop, an HSBC bank, two mobile phones stores, and a small dark den that unlocked mobile phones and sold time online upon old computers.

The community used to converge here in the town square amidst family businesses and local produce, but it's all gone. The town square was important for unifying the people but has slowly evaporated by peoples ignorance and greed.   The community has no hub anymore, and the chance meetings and synchronicities created by a community space has gone, and worse, nobody gives this a thought, Shannon thought.

She started walking home, and as she past one of the pubs, two people came out who she knew.

 "Hi Shannon, you coming into watch the England match, it's only a friendly but a good excuse for a few jars," said Darren, a guy who used to hit on her.

"Yeah, come in Shannon, not seen you for a while, and someone told me John and you are going through a tough time?" Asked Andy, a not so close friend of Johns.

Shannon started to feel sick, she could feel the energy of blind patriotism escape out the door, and she had a flash of inner knowing that being patriotic was like being in a co-dependent relationship with a selfish lover.

"Err, no thanks guys, I'm on my way home," She managed in a stony tone.

Andy looked at her like he didn't recognise her as he took a long drag on his spliff as he bowed his head to look at her face from another angle.

Shannon could feel darkness above his head start to form a cloud, one that would suck his energy and short term memory, deliver apathy, and slowdown his sharpness of mind.

"No problem Shannon, hope I can call you soon if it's true you and John aren't together," said Darren, and looked at her with desire masked as a fake appreciation of beauty.

Darren had been in the military for a few years but was kicked out for drugs.

She could see he was now hard coded with a right-wing slant on things, where hard work was the king of respect, and he had this sort of military squint, one that showed up a lack of symmetry in his face that must have come from taking so many orders.

Shannon told him silently through her eyes as she thought of a reply, *There are many who do not know they are fascists but will find it out when the time comes.*

"Don't think so Darren, have fun you guys." She said with confidence and walked away towards home, knowing that Darren and Andy where still eyeing her up as some sort of newly available flesh. Shannon shuddered inside.

Shannon walked past her old school as she neared home, and wondered why children had to go all the time.

Why not choose the lessons they liked or thrived in? Why did they have to do homework?   It feels in energy like it's just a feeder centre for capitalism and the central banks, nothing like a place of human wisdom, human endeavour, or human morals. Why spend so much time away from parents? Are parents just to clothe and feed?   How is it that humans over time have explored sciences, arts, and spirituality, but not education methods and structures that largely remain from over fifty years ago?

It was too much, she wanted to turn all this off, to stop feeling and seeing all of this.   She felt sick, like her nervous system was shaking and tearing itself apart.   But then she remembered her experience with the All Seeing Eye, and a rush of energy came over her, expanding her even more. A renewing warmth and glow came giving confidence and security.   A healthy humour rose within her and she laughed as she closed her front door.

Shannon slept long and deep, she dreamt but couldn't remember any of them upon awaking, probably because she wanted to know if she still felt so open.   She turned on Sky News, and within a few seconds she knew she was as open and sensitive as ever.   An item was showing hero worship for some British soldiers in Afghanistan, but Shannon could only feel the pain of the twenty thousand civilians who had died since the British forces had arrived there.

She ate and found some balance, then decided to go online instead of going out.   After reading some more about the Chinese five elements, she went on facebook.

Amidst the posts of cats, dinners, babies, GMO's, media lies, new age white shadow, and self elevation, a few posts caught her eye.

Carl Jung estimated that everything we feel about or see in another person is about 75% our own stuff, our shadow projected, positive and negative and has really nothing to do with the other person in reality.

What you need to realize is that a good state of soul can, in this world, go hand in hand with a feeling of deep inward disharmony, of confusion and cloudiness.

The world is getting better and worse.....but the negative has more noise.

Click, she closed the laptop, and felt drained.   There was something about Facebook that drained her, and she knew not whether it was the hooks into the CIA and NSA, the advertising bots crunching her experience, or the whole voyeuristic nature of the strange electronic portal. But she *was* drained, and slept.

*

The next day Shannon woke to missed calls from John, Darren, and Flora. She called Flora and told her she still felt wide open, and would take today's lesson off if ok. Flora was helpful and understanding and told her to take all the time she needed.

Shannon was relaxing when a text message arrived stating her car tax was overdue, and that the central computer would send her a fine in twenty four hours time if it wasn't corrected. It seemed like a small grey puff of smoke similar to ash came out of the phone as she put it down to get ready to go out again.

On the way out Shannon past a Newsagents where today's papers all stood prominently and proud in a display out the front. The energy of lies and fear frittered from them, along with a stench of a factory press and the dark emotion of the actual writers and their editors.   Each shouted prejudice, as if a corporate loudspeaker was on repeat and only audible to her ears.

In the queue at the large new centralised post office, energy started to amplify again. Shannon could see old people in the queue feeling down and pitiful at the loss of their local community post offices.   She could see the glass barriers between the clerks and people create an energetic barrier – one that sat between robotic administrators, guardians of the system, and that of the public audience, each desiring something, each desiring to jump through frustrating hoops.

"How can I help you?" The administrative humanoid said, as if she hated her job, and had no love, passion, or support for what she did.

"I need some car tax please," Said Shannon, trying to look normal, but feeling anything but.

Papers….papers…..forms…forms…..sign…..sign……..do   you have…..you need…..you need……

Was all Shannon could hear through the glass. She looked up and saw scores of small grey smoky bat-like creatures circling around behind the glass, each no bigger than a mouse. Each thriving in the order and administration, each eating and bathing in the deathlike structure within the clerks, the gatekeepers.

"I…..I….I have to go." Shannon ran out.

As Shannon's dainty jog slowed to a walk, she began to feel sick as she started to see the pain of people she passed in the street; their emotions, prejudices, their disdain, their pathetic normality in a unity of a delivered normality.

She closed her front door, and just made it to the bathroom before being sick. She hung their over the basin for a while, something was happening to her, she needed to go, to get out, to leave.

She went online to book a flight, somewhere calm, somewhere with space, but a funny trance state took hold of her, like a dream.

Love, love, a place of love, the city of love, Paris.

She clicked to book it, but then she felt the computerised greed of the Airline asking for money through multiple pages of options where it was hard to see where to say no.

Finally, Done, I fly tonight.

Shannon slept for the afternoon.

After calling a taxi, she packed lightly, and made sure she armed herself with some lavender and rosemary oils, with both generously dabbed on her temples, crown, brow, and back of her neck.

At the airport security queue she could feel the blank energy of the security staff who sat their vessels and minds upon a set of rules made up from someone else. Each help a signature of ex-military, policing, or prison work. The haze above the area was like a cloud of persecution, as if the people were all suspects, all possibly preparing to blow up a plane – all guilty until proven innocent. Babies cried, and adult groups played *who's the best sheep* – who knew the rules the most, who could advice their travel companions with their superior knowledge of what to do and when.

"Is this your bag Miss?" One grey looking man asked her.

"Yes" replied Shannon, walking over to a clear desk with him.

He rummaged for a while, then picked out the oils.

"Are these yours?"

"Yes."

"What do you use them for?"

"Different things."

"Like what, what do *you* use them for?

Shannon paused before replying, looking deeply into him, realising the question was a real curiosity from his subconscious, and he was using job's authority to know.

"They're natural liquids from the plant kingdom, safely below *your* quantity limit, what I use them for is not relevant."

Shannon was shocked at herself, at looked at him as his aura shrunk.

"Very well Miss, but mind your attitude here."

As she walked into the foray of shops and cafes, the cloud from the security area tried to follow her, to leech onto her, but she wouldn't let it with her will, and it soon found a group of young males who had been drinking to latch onto.

Shannon went into the books store, and found an array of horror, crime thriller, and celebrity autobiographies pleading to be bought. There was no art here, no message, no wisdom, just junk, so she left and went to sit at the gate.

The gate was half full, and most were on their laptops or tablets, half of which with earphones in. She could see which ones were online by some small ash coloured translucent clouds floating around the user. It was as if each IP address gave a new corner of space to some low level etheric parasites. One user had a larger cloud than others.

Once on the plane the man who had the larger cloud around him sat across, and a row in front of Shannon, and opened up his laptop again. Shannon could see the charts of the FTSE market load up. The cloud came back, floating out of the laptop. It was as if the greed and fear emotions behind the markets opened a portal of sorts, and Shannon realised this had to be an etheric reason for the large number of traders living lives of hookers and cocaine. Professional trading was a human life close to the demonic, where evocating astral parasites was easily done subconsciously because ones vibration was so close to theirs.

Once the plane was airborn, Shannon knew each breathe she was breathing would be shared with other passengers lungs, deep in their auras. She again dabbed the oils on her, and after thirty minutes she could see a light grey cloud in the cabin hopping from lung to lung. It bypassed her, and she could feel she was sharing air with three other women and an older man, even thought they were each spread out from each other. It was as if twenty or so different air streams where working in a rhythm on the plane, and vibration went to vibration, and humans of similar frequency shared the same air.

Shannon closed her eyes, and practiced remaining present for the rest of the flight.

Soon Shannon was at one of the major bus stations in the centre of Paris, waiting in line for a taxi to take her to her an apartment she had booked at random.   The bus station had junkies, drunks, and thieves milling around in the shadows.   *These places are central hubs and gateways in large affluent cities, an area of no community due to the transient energy of motion, it's no wonder this space is a magnet for those infused with astral parasites,* she thought.

The next day Shannon found herself in a dreamlike state, still wide open, and increasingly expanding. She decided to seek solace in one of the large beautiful parks.

Shannon felt underdressed, she wore loose jeans and a grey hoody, but the other women there were dressed up to the nines in expensive clothes, with many parading their babies and toddlers in posh outfits as though they were going to weddings. Shannon sat on a bench around a large pond and took it all in.

Children played together, with their mothers caring mostly for any dirt on their clothes, their over-safety, containment, and their volume levels.

That you must know what obstacles and what world-tendencies the soul you are now preparing will have to face during the next fifty years. If you teach them without any knowledge of what will soon await them, it's as if you sent them off on a journey to a country you did not know anything about, Shannon thought, not knowing if the thought was hers.

A couple of affluent women in their forties walked past, both looking at the children with disdain, willing them to be quiet.

These two are masking their despair, they've told themselves they didn't want children but this was their ultimate gift; to create, to see creation face to face, to nurture, to grow, to act selflessly, to pass on. To create the ultimate community, that of family.

Shannon began to write some notes at what she was beginning to observe and realise.

Childrearing today could be compared to a modern playground, what with its safety swings and plastic slides and soft sands everywhere. Childhood in general have gotten so manicured, structured and managed that no hint of wildness or danger remains. Whereas once children used to scamper imaginatively for hours through open fields and forests, playing at being knights or intrepid explorers, adults today organize all their activities, slicing and dicing each child's day into discrete functions, and prioritizing them based on adult opinions about which are the most important -- with safety always a top priority. Over time then, almost imperceptibly, we've become separated from the wilderness, from nature, from the curiosity of self-exploration, from creative experimentation and emotional self-expression.

Shannon could feel two of the mothers were on their cycles (it was nearly full moon). They were moody and tired.   Shannon felt sadness over how women once were in their power at this time; creative, not destructive, as it was with the witches and female occult groups, before Christianity wiped them out.   It was as if some astral parasites had come into the western world and stripped women of their power during menstruation.   But she knew it was a modern diet and materialism that was cutting them off.

Shannon walked from the park, through streets lined with old architecture. Many career types were on their way to lunch, many looking like fashion victims; the masks of today's world that were sold, worn, promoted, and agreed upon. Each on a their way to self cherishing gluttony - fuelled with expectation, with no thought for the world's problems or the souls evolution.

Shannon stopped outside a small zoo, but the pain of the animals washed out of the gates like a constant breeze. A small girl with her mother came out holding a stuffed toy of a tiger. Shannon looked into her eyes then continued to walk.

She passed a group of homeless men begging for money, but she could feel these were a now a gang of thieves looking for prey.

These are the true results of capitalism, for every winner there's a loser, she thought.

One of the gang was peering into a posh restaurant where a rich couple ate. They ignored him and etherically sent disdain, in-turn, he sent disdain back at them, and astral parasites came like ghouls out of the sky into all three of them. Shannon could see these parasites were invoked by the calls of disdain and ignorance. As they danced down they saw Shannon, but took no notice of her, and went straight into their new masters.

A large fountain appeared in the centre of a large square, enabling Shannon to feel at ease for the first time in hours. She sat on the side and placed her hand into the cool blue, and a message laced with femininity came, *Just observe Shannon, this is all happening for a reason.*

She pulled her hand out and saw a group of five tourists taking photos and aiming to be happy.

Why not create a life you don't want a holiday from? Maybe holidays are an old paradigm thing anyway, were soon people will just want to travel just to collect experiences and growth?

She walked off and got lost in some side streets of the city centre, passing more tourists, and more thoughts entered her consciousness. *Look at them, enjoying themselves just because they are in 'Paris.' Mentally geared up to enjoy themselves due to being away from their lives, but in reality they are just walking down a cold dirty street where everything is expensive.*

These thoughts kept coming in, she didn't like them, they were negative, but she knew not from where they came. They felt like *her* thoughts, but it was all so unlike, and so far from the old her.

She passed through the Jewish quarter, and as she passed a synagogue a male Jew exited and looked at her with disdain because she wasn't one of them. Shannon laughed inside herself as many of these people thought they really were descendents from the tribe of Israel in the old testament, The Chosen People. Again a thought came.

Isis-Ra-El, the bible really spoke of a mystery cult that lived through ancient Egypt.

She walked on and came to Notre Dame, the massive cathedral awash with alchemical and gothic symbolism. She entered and immediately felt an old energy of power and corruption. Some children were involved in a small service and she could feel the pain from their souls, they didn't want to be there.

Two monks stood watching her, they could feel she was open and empathic. She stared back at them, awash with thoughts.

When you're engaged in your blind compassion, you rarely show any anger, not only do you believe that compassion has to be gentle, but you also are frightened of upsetting anyone, especially to the point of their confrontation. This is reinforced by your judgment of anger, especially in its more fiery forms, as something less than spiritual; something to be equated with ill will, hostility, and aggression; something that shouldn't be there if you were being truly loving. In blind compassion you don't know how to, or won't learn how to, say 'no' with any real power, avoiding confrontation at all costs and, as a result, enabling unhealthy patterns to continue. Your 'yes is then anaemic and impotent, devoid of the impact it could have if you were also able to access a clear, strong 'no' that emanated from your core. Blind compassion confuses anger with aggression, forcefulness with violence, judgment with condemnation, exaggerated tolerance with caring, and spiritual correctness with moral maturity.

They looked at her with surprise, but a deep hidden hatred emanated from them that they couldn't stop. Shannon walked away from them, and continued to feel the energy in the Catholic Cathedral, and residual energy of all the ritual that had been played out within this building.

What happens through this kind of magic here? By ritual, sung and spoken in a dead language, by specially-prepared music, by perfumes, by the mudras of priests, and by magnetized waters and other preparations, the faithful are brought into a trance-like state, a state of negativity; lack, guilt, fear, and shame. In this state, ethers are drawn from the auras of the faithful by nature-spirits, which they are led to believe are 'angels.' But they are really just a connected to a large control-spirit, so the faithful, after a few of these magic applications, are bound with their entire being; and it would take them a tremendous effort to escape from this grip.

This Catholic religion even lays hold of the children in the family, binding them from the time of their birth until the hours of death. When death approaches, it even ensures their captivity *afterwards, because on the other side of the veil, the natural hierarchy is just as well-organized and strong and has just as much power over its prisoners as it does here. It receives the dead who are spiritually deaf, blind and unable to gain any consciousness of the True Light.*

This Catholic herd is enlarged by means of missionary work, mass baptisms, mass communions and processions, often move the unknowing to laughter. However, it is no laughing matter, for these are serious mass deprivations of liberty, bound in this fashion, they will be forced, upon their return to earth-life, to be born into a Catholicism, The circuit of imprisonment is neatly closed.

People should stay out of the churches. There is great danger here. Far more danger than can be imagined.

Shannon was almost in a fear state due to these thoughts, but compassion overrode it. She walked to an encased large book, and was drawn to the paragraph near the top on the right.

Do not be afraid of those who kill the body but cannot kill the soul. Instead, fear the one who is able to destroy both soul and body in hell. Matthew 10:28

One of the monks from earlier startled her as he peered over her shoulder, "You see something in our sacred place of worship that startles you my young female wanderer?" He whispered.

She looked him in the eyes, and sent him a silent thought form.

Magic can only be liberating if it is applied from within, from inner Knowledge, in selfless service; when it is an act of the new will ignited from divine will. All other magic is for control.

She cared not if he actually received it, but she knew she had left the thought form there, hovering like a bubble.....until the next ritual of control probably cleared it.

She went back to the dull apartment, and slept for fourteen hours.

The next day Shannon felt more dreamlike, and more empathic. But she also felt brave, as though she wished to feel as much as she could this day, and cared not for herself. She could hide in her dream-like state she thought.

She walked to the famous Père Lachaise Cemetery, and as she approached, four large blackbirds flew from a tree and squawked at her. She continued, and as she got to the entrance, an energy of death and evil came over her. Dark occultists, Gothic Romanticists, Alchemists, Royalty, and powerful people were all buried here, along with some famous artists. But the place had been used as a tourist attraction, a kind of theme park for the dead.

From some dead soil, eight large ghouls rose up and stared at her. Each were about four meters high, each like an ash-black colored haze of smoke, each in a shape of a deformed and skewed overweight humanoid who had been maimed in a battle.

They each threw dark etheric ash balls at her, and two hit her, sending her to the ground. *Fuck, I gotta get out of here.*

Shannon ran across the busy road and towards the nearest Metro station. She turned back and saw that five of them couldn't get out of the cemetery, another two couldn't get across the road, but one was thudding itself down the road towards her, in a steady but slow stride, that was more like a jogger limping. Naturally, none of the other humans could see this ghoul stomping down the road towards her.

Just before she got to the steps heading down to the Metro, she grabbed a bunch of flowers from a florist, and scattered them around the Metro's entrance. A women shouted at her to pay, but Shannon was gone down the steps, two at a time, and ran onto the train awaiting, with no care for where it was going.

Shannon sat and closed her eyes, and started to feel the damage in her energy from the balls of etheric ash.

She opened them a minute later to a voice coming from a plasma screen showing the news.

On an underground train? Each segment was ultimately either a corporate advert, social engineering, or an item coating an interest rate, inflation, utility, or currency market change.

She looked around the carriage and could see the workers and business men aiming to ingest these messages with accuracy and passivity. But she could feel that workers and tax were not really needed anymore, as the central banks now created money from nothing. That there was an interest rate apartheid, were workers needed to borrow at high interest rates, but city financiers' borrowed at no interest.

Their minds are tricked and veiled, and so are their five senses, and those behind the curtain know the art of keeping people penned into a little box so they can control them, and allow the feeding of their energies by energy parasites.

She then saw small etheric critters latched onto most of the people in the carriage, ash coloured or dark grey, some like bats, some like small trolls or orcs, none any bigger than thirty centremetres, but each feeding on the energy of the human host. As the train stopped at the next stop, some jumped from one person to another. One tall businessman, who obviously held a lot of power and control immediately had about ten jump onto him and feed. He knew not, and made a call on his phone, and one even came out of the small speaker into his ear.

It was those with anxiety, fear, restriction, and suppressed emotional pain that had the most critters, and many even latched onto bright fluorescent lights.

A thought came upon her. *Complete absence of all power to concentrate thought, to follow an argument, to formulate a Will, to hold fast an opinion or a course of action, or even keep a solemn oath, mark indelibly those who have thus lost parts of their souls. These will become food for those from lesser places.*

She stood up to depart at the next stop, and all the critters stopped feeding and looked at her, they each hissed in unison. Shannon sent love and each cowered behind their human host. She ran up the stairs of the station, were she could now see critters attached to billboards, newspapers, and non organic food.

As she walked another street she could see most humans with astral critters, especially those in false decadence and fake elegance, those who walked around like fashion models but in reality lived in a tiny expensive rental apartment, devoid of any true expression of self.

The occult roads of Paris enabled these critters to move faster - looking for hosts, and attaching to any greedy or manipulative thoughts. Seeking media delivered group think, and those in routine where the habit defined the self.

The humans were doing the critters work, making the world more chaotic and corrupt, in turn allowing more critters to be evoked.

Shannon saw souls who wouldn't go any further as they were owned by larger critters, those souls who would be eaten upon death of the vessel. This was the end of the road for them unless some miraculous mass transformation ensued to break the etheric pact.

One man in the street coming to pass her had a swarm of critters attached. It was too much for her, she had no way to defend herself, she had to feed his ego or many would jump onto her. She quickly look flattered to his sexual glance of desire and this was enough, it gave him what he needed, and the critters reattached to him and forgot about her. She knew she had to give to his ego as she couldn't win.

As she walked more she developed a technique to stop any critters looking at her.

She offered her divinity humbly to whoever she passed with critters, whatever she had, she offered it in an empty state of non fear. This protected her.

The evening hues were drawing in casting diagonal orange shadows down the streets, and outside an organic market she saw some flyers for events. One caught her eye.

Sacred Shamanic Sex – Learn conscious sensuality Level 1. She almost laughed when the thought overcome her. *Shamanism isn't a sexual act, shamanism is a voyage of healing far away from the physical. The most sacred sex is the one where both parties are so open and so full of love that they gladly invoke the forces of creation to conjure a soul to arrive here. No techniques, no theory, and no mental manipulation of sexual energy can be a substitute for the force of this invocation, for it invokes the forces of creation to pass through them, and that is really shamanic. Heheh, Sacred Shamanic Sex….with condoms….hehe.*

The second flyer Shannon saw pulled her in right away.

Tibetan Bowls, tonight, in the east cave of Parque de Pierre.

Twenty minutes later Shannon was in the park making her way to the east cave, and in this vibrant beautiful nature of trees and lush grass, she was able to sooth, heal, and have her senses put back in order somewhat.

She saw a cat, exactly like the one in the barn. It chased two flies, two small manifest critters of dirt and frustration

Shannon stood in the cave amongst a circle of eight others. Not one had any critters, and she could see each were empathic to a level too. *Wow, it could be so easy here, we could have attained another golden age centuries ago,* She thought.

After she laid down on the prepared mat, the bowls started to resonate within her. The cave soon disappeared and she was in an astral place of ancient resonance, a resonance that could invoke, and evoke. A resonance that raised the frequency of the body to allow healing, journeying, and ascendance to a higher realm in the inner worlds.

Shannon flew in the astral. Images, memories, and symbols came and went, then emotions and animals came and went. All the while the bowls lifted her, enabling her to glide upon the sound, and linking her soul that was travelling directly to the sound. An astral violet cloud appeared below her and she journeyed upon it, it was linked to the very resonance of the bowls themselves.

"Shannon, over here, come here, Shannon, over here, come here."

The voice increased in volume. Shannon felt a familiar energy from the resonance of the voice and glided her violet cloud towards it.

"I'm coming," She replied.

Shannon then found herself in a small astral cave temple lit by three thick candles that flickered in the small breeze. Opposite her was a lady sitting cross legged with a hood over her bowed head so Shannon could not see her face.

"Sit young one, heheh," She commanded.

Shannon sat, and as she looked around the lady spoke again.

"I allow you to ask a questions dear one. You may feel it too Shannon, but know that us here together was prepared a long time ago."

Shannon tried to see the lady's face, but the lady bowed her head a little more and adjusted her hood to show it was disrespectful at this junctia to look.

"Shannon, ask!"

"Er, ok then ma'am...thank you......these critters I can now see, are they real?"

"The Gnostics knew of these in depth, and so did many other ancient traditions. We could call them demons or Jinn, but I prefer to call the Archons. The Archons transform us to be like them as they cannot come to this frequency physically. They have no souls and are jealous of man. We are at a time where it is not only the fact most people are locked into the mundane with no desire to control traits or their illusory personality, we are at a time where parasitical forces are chomping away at most people....without them even knowing it. There's a two way feed is going on, man is greedy, gluttonous, and lustful, and then the archons feed and coerce their hosts to do more. This is how psychopaths and sociopaths are created, and now one in seven humans are hosting archons, and this is not even to mention the Aeons which man links too, but that is for another time. Shannon, sensitivity is a sign of life. Better hurt than hardened. We are currently in the midst of the greatest epidemic sickness known to humanity. The madness is so pervasive that it has become normalized. Humans have become conditioned to accept as normal the fact that they are in an endless war. I bow to those who keep their hearts open when it's most difficult, those who refuse to keep their armour on any longer than they have to, those who recognize the courage at the heart of vulnerability. After all the misguided warriors destroy each other, the open-hearted will inherit the earth.....ah, we have no more time, for the eye is coming closer."

The lady pulled down her hood.   It was another version of Shannon, her higher self maybe, or her from another time in the illusory future.   Whatever she was began to fade, and the whole cave temple began to fade into gold dust that swirled in geometric patterns.

Then she floated up in this dark space, and began to feel less earth bound. She could feel cosmic energy, and soft charge from the power of creation. Symbols began to float past her, Sanskrit, Hebrew, Mandalas, and then symbols she had never seen came – but she knew through feeling they were part of the fabric and make-up of the earth reality.

She floated upwards in vibration, expanding her being further, and then new symbols came that felt even more unfamiliar, and in their background she could see galaxies and nebulae.

Then everything formed into a large eye, and she merged with it. Once again she was the all seeing eye and below her a large pyramid formed, half white, and half black – containing all images, archetypes, and forces. She could feel the power and harmony of the universe, but a small part of *her* still existed in this place, and she ground into this place of *Shannon*, and she gracefully asked;

"Who am I?"

 "I am the absolute," Came the reply.

"What time is it?"

"The time is now," Came the reply.

"What do I need?"

"Nothing that I don't already have," Came the reply.

 "Why am I here?"

 "To remember who I am," Came the reply.

Then she felt love, like that of a spring flower, that of a mother's touch, that of a couple kissing after an initial bond, that of a step into freedom, that of a dew drop, all she could feel was love. Within this love she could feel the forces of creation, will, and true knowledge, Gnosis. She could feel the structures within all of the realities in the inner and outer universe all at once.

As she was about to explode into these forces, about to cease to be a spark of consciousness, but the eye and pyramid faded slowly away from her, allowing her to separate once again. Shannon took on the form of a human shape, her astral body, and started to fall gently downward, past galaxies, nebulae, intelligence, and symbols.

As she floated through the milky way galaxy towards the outer limb, she closed in on the solar system hosting earth, and started to feel the heavy energies of the planetary intelligences.

Then as she fell further, past the celestial bodies in the solar system, she neared earth, and could feel giant pillars and guardians.

She could see forty intelligences around the earth, each feminine, and each a separate force of virtue.

Then she could feel a hundred lower intelligences, separate from the forty she just passed, these were Aeons, each an energetic force humans fed from and latched too; Lust, Greed, Drugs, Alcohol, Sadism, Fame, Power, Pride, Prejudice, Gambling, High Tech Gadgets, and the like.

Shannon could see each living characteristic as a deity, and knew at that moment that man's thoughts were often not their own. Rather that oftentimes they were simply responding to powerful impulses continuously sent forth by the many Aeons that act as parasites upon unwitting humanity. Shannon could feel that the reason man responded to these *Aeonic* impulses is because somewhere in man's aura, many carry vibrations of a similar nature. So in many cases, Man does not live, he is lived.

Shannon could now see the critters, archeons, and aeons were all linked, part of a hierarchy.

"Why did you pick me to show me all this?" She whispered to herself.

"Simply, you were nearest." Came the reply, from where, she knew not.

She fell in vibration, and her expansion was condensing into her as she fell into the sphere of the four elements of earth. Earth was the mother, the cradle, Sophia, and she floated in the bliss of feminine design, creation, nurture, and abundance.

Then a voice came, one she knew. It was strangely like the Shaman from the ayahuasca ceremony a week or so ago. Then she heard the voice of two of the people who were there as well.

A surge of energy hit Shannon, as if she was forced through an hourglass then an eye of a needle.

She opened her eyes, and she was back in the barn.

She had never left.

She hadn't gone to Paris, she hadn't gone home, she hadn't gone to town, she hadn't opened her eyes, or even sat up.

In an earthbound perspective she was only *gone* a few hours.

Shock would have grabbed her, but she was still floating through the astral fog back into this reality.

Some of those in the circle were speaking, starting to share their experiences, or just to say something they felt.

Shannon could just about hear one person's words through the evaporating haze,....... "Dear mother goddess, unknowable father,

The All, I offer you my divinity. Please grant me clemency and salvation, new humility, and new dignity. Please allow me solidity, balance, health, and protection in all the four elements. I serve through your abundance, beauty, wisdom, and truth. I am loved by you more than I can ever conceive or understand.....Amen, Eheiheh, Eheiheh, Eheiheh."

Shannon floated off a little as the haze thickened a little, but soon she caught some more words from another ".....be in the world, not of the world."

"And you Shannon, do you have anything to share?" Said the shaman.

She pushed through the pulsing astral haze, to try and meet with the earthly words.......but was far from being able to focus, let alone speak. She started to be sick. It was all too much.

Earth Splitz Reset

The invited creator beings (or maybe one should say, *energies of combined intelligence groupings*) turned up at the astral temple as requested. Each ready to take part in the high level meeting about what to do with Earth. This was called as some rumours were starting to spread in many quadrants about maybe resetting, or even destroying the earth experiment, as for the third time, it wasn't working. The type of beings present in this meeting were known as orders or hosts to many humans, those overseen by archangels in some traditions. This meeting was required to output some firm conclusions and actions, or the archons would twist humanity towards even more soulless greed and violence, and in turn, destroy Gaia even more.

Melachim was chairing the meeting, and it was flowing along nicely with the opening formalities, when out of apparently nowhere, a small human - ablaze with violet, was seen wandering around the temple, as small as a mouse. He was shining, but walking around as though lost in a giants house.

Some of the beings on the edge of the temple darted out to see the Lion and Tiger headed guardians standing post outside the entrance. They were ok and knew of no intruders. He certainly didn't come in this way.

The temple went quiet, and Melachim started to laugh loudly, "Rahahah, what are you doing here little one? Have you got lost?"

The human increased in strength and bravery, "I would like some questions answered," he said, almost commandingly, as he waltzed with confidence to the centre of the temple.

"Rahahahaa," bellowed Melachim and others, and then waved a finger.

The temple morphed into a Gladiators auditorium, with the meeting participants lofted into the surrounding spectator areas, leaving the human soul left alone in the middle looking somewhat bewildered.

A Hydra appeared in a fizz from out of nowhere, and started to hiss as it attacked the human. The Hydra was the pet guardian of this astral dimension, here to stop any humans or other lesser beings from coming to such places uninvited. The human was shocked at the act of aggression, and peeled away and rolled as the serpent's seven heads each attacked with their own techniques, feigns, and strategies.

The human then started to use his own magic; pentagrams, beams of gold and white, and violet dots all flew in magical geometric patterns from his hands. The Hydra seemed angrier, and more determined to rid this curious human from this realm, and more importantly, this trajectory changing meeting!

The battle continued, with momentum flowing from one to other, but often returning back to a knife edge. The creator beings had never seen this within a meeting before. Then light and then the shapes of elves appeared in the humans aura he tripled in size. Out of his palms flew thousands of almond blossoms straight into the eyes of the Hydra's multiple dragon heads. The hydra span in panic, jumped, and in a blaze of gold light in the air, transformed into an almond seed. The human then shrunk, jogged to the centre, and calmly caught the seed as it fell.

"Now, my questions please." He said with respect.

"Rahahahhaa," beamed Melachim, as a vibrating, hush fell across the auditorium, almost creating a buzzing sound.

"Fire away little one, but remember, asking the proper question is the central action of transformation. The properly shaped question always emanates from an essential curiosity. Questions are the keys that cause the secret doors to swing open." Melachim could at will create another thousand Hydra's, but this human had earned some fruits.

"Sir, could you please tell me the true ancient history of humanity. For we are in amnesia, we don't know our true history of where we came from, and I believe this subconsciously is the cause of much of our worldly pain." The human said with humility.

Melachim peered forward, "Rahaha, many wiser minds than you have asked lesser questions and got no answer." Melachim then jangled some keys in front of him.

"These keys are not for you my little friend, but instead I will give you a little gift due to the pleasure of watching you with the Hydra." Melachim waved a finger and the human flew off out of the auditorium, as the space then slowly morphed back into the temple.

The human spent the next human hours in the energy of patience, the root of the energy, and the benefits and teachings of patience. It was exactly what he needed, but he would never forget the auditorium, most of all, how the beings there had the overwhelming feeling that a thousand years in earth time was but a mere speck of dust to them.

Melachim shuffled some papers as though nothing had happened, "Ok, let's get started."

The meeting went on and on, round and round in circles for a while, but what was slowly being agreed upon, was that earth had become a dumping ground for souls. That the earth contained a much too wide a' contrast of souls at different stages of evolution.

Life for many humans had become a futile attempt to become secure in a dimension that was intrinsically insecure.

Too many evolved souls were putting up with too much darkness and dense resonance.

Too many lesser evolved souls were experiencing too much light and subtle resonance they could not experience.

Neither were getting what they needed. It didn't work. Souls would need to be moved.

The meeting calmly continued. Each being present presented case studies and ideas, other beings darted off pursuing research into other worlds, and how things had worked or not worked before. Others created mini-astral-prototype-worlds.

The meeting continued.

*

It was agreed. Earth would be split. It would be multiplied into more identical looking Earths (but into different worlds or *reality constructs* as they said at the meeting). Each of the new Earth's would have different virtues and laws. Two more earth worlds would exist at a higher vibration, and two more earth worlds at a more dense vibration.

To move the seventy percent of souls that were earmarked to be moved, an event would have to occur to create the physical deaths in the current, *unique* Earth. This would ensure the remaining thirty percent on the original earth would believe the others had 'died' (though death was seen as a silly unevolved human notion amongst these beings, because energy can only transform).

The rest of the trajectories regarding events, design, and designations were all decided upon, and then swiftly put into action on the peak of the winter solstice.

*

A large X-flare exploded from the Sun to help release its eleven years of twisting electromagnetics and electricity.   Just nine minutes later, a coronal mass ejection quickly followed. It took only one hundred and fourteen minutes to reach earth and play havoc with the earths electromagnetic shield.

It wiped out all electrical components on the planet and immediately charged all of the particles in the southern hemispheres of Earth's inner and outer cores. This commenced a three hour crust displacement of six degrees. Whole continents slowly moved and rotated in unison. From a humans perspective, the sunrise and sunset would never be at the same points again, neither would north or south.   When the crust displacement stopped, the three hundred and twenty six million trillion gallons of water in the seas started to move and gain momentum, In a dance of seeking equilibrium.   A super Tsunami built up and swept across most of the Americas from the pacific. Other related tsunamis wiped out anything within a hundred miles of near all coastlines on the planet, up to five hundred meters.

Sixty Eight percent of all human souls left the reality during the crust displacement, due to the earthquakes and tsunamis it caused.

The world had changed. Forever. All electronic data had gone, electricity itself was gone, and the car engine had gone. After an eerie calm had restored to the atmosphere, only thirty or so percent of human souls remained on the earth. Only Madrid and Berlin out of all cities in the world were left relatively in one piece.

*

Earth was affectively reset, and labelled by the creator beings as Earth three, because two more sat above it in vibration, in a faster frequency, plus two more sat below it, in a more dense frequency.

The humans remaining would morn, suffer, and slowly rebuild in a new way, into a new direction.   The catastrophe had came, as it always did, so that Man might learn from the experience.

Those who stayed were chosen to.   They were those who experienced much pain within the toxic and planet-destroying, western system.   They were humans that didn't *do* much to change anything, but were being terribly real beings within a false world. Neutral.   So they stayed with the pain of their losses to shake them into action....it was hoped.   For remember, free-will, the ultimate gift, was still prevalent in each human, and the virtues and laws hard wired into the reality construct were left completely untouched.

This world was actually deemed a hellworld by the creator beings for millennia. This was because the more hellish a person was, the more they were falsely rewarded within the dense and external; decadence, luxury, and lavishness.   Those with ethics and no desire for control or power, had been placed upon the sidelines, but now ethics from free-will had a blank canvas, an opportunity to return.   No longer would the adults need to subconsciously toughen up their children to face a cruel and heartless world.

This opportunity had more probability of succeeding this time around as the humans with psychopathic and greedy tendencies from being riddled with astral parasites had left this realm to move to one of the new others

Earth was effectively reset, and would be seen from now on by the orders of Intelligences behind the veil as Earth-Three.

*

Only the animals inhabited the *next* Earth construct for the quiet few days before they came. Then in a silent expanding, and emanating second or two, hundreds of millions of humans of all ages appeared, as if from nowhere.   Melting in through a golden shimmer shaped in a human form.

This was what the creator beings called Earth-Two, resting at a higher frequency than the original.

Those that were moved here were souls that were kind and generous.   Those more in service to others than service to self. Souls that had already done much self work in past Earth carnations.   Those that didn't radically change too much, but quietly brightened up peoples days, and simply gave. This was not to mean they were all similar because they weren't, but they had proved to be morally superior to those now in the lower three worlds to this one.   This is not about better or worse, but there is objectiveness in a souls evolution, no matter what any communist new ager may have one think.

Each found themselves in the same location they were in *before* the natural disaster, and each could remember their experience of it, but each felt it as a dream in memory. They physical eyes told them nothing appeared to have changed, no tsunamis, no earthquakes, no pole rotation. But each could feel it. All was more sensitive, like someone had turned up an amplifier just a notch on colour, feelings, emotion, and therefore, pain and care, or as it became more commonly known here; suffering and healing.

The energy of virtues had all changed a little too. Positive virtues each had more of an energy signature, one would be able to feel them more - each virtue like a unique subtle train of cotton wool picking them up once one sat within.   Vices and anger would broadcast that a place or person needed some attention. Like an etheric emergency beacon.

Within the first minute of their arrival, the creator beings placed the same small love tinged thought forms into each person. They each now knew, though they didn't know how or where from, that something divine had occurred, that some intelligent intervention had moved them. They also knew that their loved ones and other souls they would never see again, had also been moved where they needed to go. There was no pain to be felt, only celebration for those they once knew and whom they shared an experience of reality and life with.

They also arrived with less amnesia of humanities past, they had been given a gift. The knowledge of ancient civilisations. Their history, timelines, how's, why's, and even some technologies, all reaching back as far as 14,000BC. This was a real game changer as religion and technology completely changed in this moment.

The motion of life started again.

Nationalities disappeared, as it was known nationalism was just a form of insanity, one that could give launch to its dark cult; Patriotism, the virtue of the vicious.

Travel by new technologies sprouted, and the use of money was immediately felt to be silly.

The thought of *having* to work was known to be silly too. Work was the source of much misery in the old world. Much pain came from competitive markets, so in order to stop suffering, they decided to stop working. This did not mean to stop doing things. It meant creating a new way of life based on play; in other words, a lucid conviviality of innovation, collaboration, and creation. They called for a collective adventure in generalised joy and freely interdependent exuberance.

Play that wasn't passive.

They felt they all needed some rest time, to settle, but once recovered from *that* reality, that employment-induced exhaustion, they knew nearly every human here wanted to act.

The old world was like a gravity hole that sucked the vitality from life, and was left undistinguished from mere survival.

The people started to balance time between inner world and outer world, more focus on ones evolution, the species evolution, and into ones purpose. More focus upon ones shadow when it arose. It was almost like planetary shadow cult aiming to transform the shadow individually and collectively. They all knew after a short time the philosophies of the shadow; that a beam of light only appears bright in contrast to the dark shadows which envelop it. That the same beautiful beam of light would seem insignificant in a bright, sunny atmosphere. That when the shadows of darkness are known, one is given a gift; the ability to see the beautiful contrast of the light to the darkness.

Popularity and prestige started to depend upon little, save how much one did to help others, and children were rewarded for good more than punished for bad. It was looked at as folly to demand children to be obedient, needy, passive, and weak willed, only to tell them the opposite in adulthood.

After some time, the humans from twenty-one to thirty-three were seen as *the* master innovators. They were given the platform and support to make decisions as they were so fresh and full of new life and ideas. They knew not of the old ways.

The older generation were analysed and contemplated regarding the decisions they'd made in previous years, to see clearly the state of society they had left for them.

There was no punishment or rules in this, it was just like a wave, and the younger adults would always ride the crest of it. In this, the elders were always respected and known to be the greatest advisors, for whatever mistakes they made were understood, never judged.

Children and youth from eight years old were looked to for ideas, for their imaginations had no limits. And young adults would each year add and remove words within the planetary dictionary, adding words to create more depth in communication that lent itself to more evolution, progress, and understanding. Words of toxicity that created dark mental patterns were slowly removed.

The old earth worked on the notion that when everything fell into place, peace would be found, on Earth-Two they knew that when peace was found, everything would fall into place.

They also knew there were other realities more enjoyable than this one, so they set themselves up to thrive here, and set the canvas for life to flourish and evolve. This was a great stop in the bigger life.

*

They arrived in Earth-Four much the same way as they appeared in Earth-Two.   Hundreds of millions of souls each appearing through a this time, smoky-grey shimmer, shaped as a human body.

The hundreds of millions of arrivals were those who were in service to self. They who had played the game of western capitalism well, and became *that* false archetype of *success*. Those driven by greed and a quest for power and control.

People who cherished the self. Those with the classic traits of psychopaths: superficial charm, grandiosity, and self-importance; a need for constant stimulation; a penchant for lying, deception and manipulation; and the incapacity for remorse or guilt. All those ethics imbedded within the multi-national corporations and men of power and control.

Those with the beliefs that personal style and personal advancement, mistaken for individualism, were the same as democratic equality. Those who celebrated synthetic over authentic, image over substance, and illusion over truth.

Many others who arrived were like sheep before; believing in and buying into a media induced reality. Defending the status quo, living like robots without any soul. Funny really, as in the old Earth, this was admired, sold, sought after, even fought for, and a desired catch for the opposite sex. But here, in Earth-Four, well, it was different.

*

For starters they were told nothing. They could each really feel the *natural* disaster as a strong memory; the pain, desperation, confusion, chaos, and bewilderment gripped each. But their eyes told them nothing had happened. No damage or physical change was evident. It was as if a flash of light had occurred, and now many people they knew had just gone! This created confusion and even some madness.

The fabric of reality had some small integral changes they wouldn't at first notice. Gravity was one and a half percent heavier, and the weather system was tweaked to be a little more grey and rainy. Dogs were a little more aggressive, cats a little less friendly, and flies more like mosquitoes.

But the world hadn't changed from the old paradigm. Electricity still existed, trains still ran, and the illusory solidity of the system remained; money, traffic tickets, taxation, and the military. The people still held their jobs, and the stock markets still moved in their algorithmic greed and fear based cycles. The energy of dog eat dog was turned up, and respect was gained by working so hard one was stressed or physically battered. Or Both.

But it was all in order, it was just a grouping of all the people whose minds and souls weren't ready for the love world. They just had to experience more pain here, for lifetimes if needed, but sooner or later that spark of divine essence would potentially arise, that cosmic bolt that would awake them.

*

They appeared in Earth-Five through hazy outlines. The rapists and murderers, the military personnel, the violent and the abusers. The oppressors, and the leaders and creators of oppression. Those that thought they had a right to get whatever they desired - by belittling and destroying those around them, including family and friends; to make money, to create power, to create comfort.

The banking elite, the politicians, and many CEOs and Directors. Those void of empathy or compassion.

They were told nothing.

The planet was really multiple locked down mega-cities controlled by artificial intelligence, and they were the cattle. The beauty of nature was taken away from them, and an electronic synthetic control grid sat in its place. For this was the evolutional trajectory they were paving a path for, and now they were fast forwarded to taste the fruits of the roots they'd spent years planting and nurturing.

The fabric of the reality had changed, weather was polluted and there was less daylight, and almost daily, an archon or two could come into this reality frequency and maim a human or three - in broad pollute-light.

Sex was difficult, genetics were changed so a women could not easily get moist, and man was changed so it was a low probability of getting hard.   This slowed down the realisation of spiritual energy by nearly cutting off the twin sister; sexual energy.

Love was so void in this reality that men and women were rarely partners or co-habiting.   There was little creativity, variety, openness, or loving kindness.

Nations within nations existed within the electronic one world government. It exuded top down control from its upside-down pyramid, stamping each human with electronic DNA tags, and tagging rare babies at their increasingly common, artificial laboratory conceptions.

Disease and illness that slowed people down had increased, and to combat this, humans had started to merge with machine, shutting down emotions even more.

Technologically based wars increased, as did human death, only for those to reincarnate here again, often within an automated DNA breeding station.

A new disease came where some people were born mentally old, and then mentally grew in reverse towards childhood, with the body growing as normal. Chaos reigned.

A new illness increased where a human became under the mental delusion they were the only person here, the only soul here within an illusory hell world, where they had to work it out to escape. The Illness of mega-narcissism.

Many of those here had jumped from the animal kingdom too quick and were not ready for the Earth-Three, they had become dark and demonic, and this place was to create the equilibrium in energy from the imbalance caused, actuated, and lived.

The spark of divinity was still there, but only an eightieth of one percent awakened this, and somehow evolved out of this reality upon their death. The rest reincarnated here.   Nineteen and a half percent became much more chaotic within this reality, and upon death, they lost their divine spark and merged into a demonic being behind the veil.

Earth-Five was the last place to save the soul, and ironically it was the toughest place to do so.

Suffering is part of purification.

A sword needs friction to sharpen, and a tree needs deep dark soil to grow roots.

The Great Work of Liberation must be done from below upwards if it's to be truly redemptive. It cannot be done by starting from above. If this were possible, this Work would have been completed centuries ago. This is why life is so precious. It's because one only has a few short earth-years to locate Truth, recognize it and, in faith and longing, use that Truth to awaken That Which Sleeps Within.

*

Those destined for Earth-One went to a place of pure light haze. A soft and milky white, gold, and violet dance of arcs and spirals, tinged with a feeling of unconditional love. Many must had thought they had died, but they hadn't – they were in a celestial transit of sorts.

The soft hearted introverts, the creative's who spread a positive and helpful message, the freethinkers, the black-sheep, and those innovating and pioneering against the grain into the new. Those who had glimpsed behind the veil, those who sacrificed much to strive towards selfhood, those who knew and respected the nature spirits, those loving the earth and animals, and those who had healed. And surprising to many, those who faced evil in the world, those who researched and dug into the shadows, and brought them out of the human subconscious into the light.

Each of these nine hundred million souls listened as the unified messages came, as though each sound of resonance was danced upon by soft angelic energy.   They were told a little about allot; about the veil, humanities past, the moving of souls, and dimensions. But much was not told, for the veil would have to stay down.

Each was then shown the purest forms of humility, softness, and compassion. No human visuals or moving images, just the root energies the core feelings were within them and around them, as though the only *things* in the universe were these three overlapping and weaving energies. Almost like these virtues were angels themselves and they lived within them.

This experience lasted four human hours.

They each appeared on Earth-One through a white-gold shimmer outline – that felt like a container of pure bliss. The Earth was natural, all the old towns, cities, airports, hospitals, schools, sports stadiums, and industrialisation had all vanished, with no traces of them ever being there.

The earth was clean again, renewed, alive, thriving.

It was a blank canvas, save for the nature-settlements sporadically located in places of beauty near clean water springs, streams and rivers. Natural domes and pod houses were clumped together in a weave of vines, leaves, branches, soil, and clay, as though someone or something had modified nature somehow.

The human bodies were a little different too, it frayed at the edges in a gradient, for example skin had no definitive edge or end, there was about half a centremeter of blend between the body and space.   This took some getting used to, and was caused by the whole reality construct vibrating at a fast frequency.

In this reality, feelings and emotions could be felt more, anger and pain would show up like beacons, and the whole reality was background coated In humility, kindness, and compassion due to their experience in transit.

Each human had the power to manifest things out of the ether or to make things move, but It would mean three people agreeing, and then the three of them meditating for twenty four minutes. It became a magical reality of mindfulness, collaboration, and creation.

Also humans could travel in what became known as a *whisp*. One could meditate for twenty four minutes, then dart their vessel at a hundred miles an hour, for up to an hour. If going further, one could meditate, dart, meditate, dart, and keep going until ones meditation was not solid enough.

They couldn't bump into things or each other while *darting* as their vessel became more or less dematerialised.

Sophia's correction was here in this place, a golden age. Archons could still come into this frequency, but nine times out of ten it was easily dealt with by the human's healing modalities.

They knew this was Earth-One, the springboard out of this cycle. They knew they were close to the liberation of density, of hard duality. Those who meditated could see their past lives and soul story, and could use that knowledge to greater effect here – to rebalance past shortcomings to give greater chance of escape.

Most here knew that the greatest gift they could give to somebody was one's own personal development. The old earth had a philosophy of, *If you will take care of me, I will take care of you*, but here it was flipped into, *I will take care of me for you, if you will take care of you for me.*

Children were bought up to be compassionate, empathic, and healing, and many aspired to be seers, shaman, and creators, with their imaginations encouraged and coaxed.

The elderly were looked to for wisdom and stories, and they knew the afterlife awaiting them was created and connected from and to ones inner world beliefs, imagery, and knowledge.   That the vibration of this imagery and form would be placed in a degree of light or dark depending on one's actions and thoughts in this life.

When their time arrived and they transitioned from the material-sphere, it was their vibration that would determine where they went next. If they were earth-focused, they would head off to the reflection-sphere where dissolution of the personality and a return trip on the wheel of death and Rebirth would await. Conversely, if they transitioned after awakening their Divine-Spark, having endeavoured to live from the soul, they would not head off to the ordinary reflection-sphere but would instead journey to a realm of light. There would be no dissolution of the personality, no forced return to the material-sphere, only a continuation of the glorious process of transfiguration that was begun while on earth.

*

A soul could affectively move between the five earths due to it's evolution, and even spin out of the bottom of Earth-Five, or leap out of the top from Earth-One......or flitter in one, and get relegated or promoted.   All was possible.

New neutral souls evolved from the animal kingdom would incarnate into Earth-Three, and highly evolved souls that travelled around the galaxy, or even universe, could choose to incarnate in any of the worlds to learn or teach.

The creators had labelled Earth-One as insight, the second as yearning for salvation, the third as self surrender, the fourth as new attitudes, and the fifth as liberation

The creator beings wouldn't have to meddle with the five earths for many millennia, this was a good fitting solution for the horrific problems the old Earth faced.

Galactic Butterflies

After the ayahausca was downed, the candles went off, and someone out of the thirty or so people started banging a drum slowly.

Oh dear, a death ceremony, what am I doing here? I thought to myself in a cheeky giggle, one that reminded me of adolescent mischief.   It was my first time taking aya (through a synchronistic invite at a waterfall in the Himalayas), and I started to feel darkness and fear, transmuting the warm feeling of apprehension and boyish excitement into terror.   A terror that was coming out of the dark, from within and around the little green and blue dots that were starting to dance upon a black background, a background with energy of the void starting to resonate loudly.

Two snakes formed out of the dots and came out of the darkness towards me, each thick, colourful, and long, and they coiled themselves around me like I was their hunted prisoner.   Slick, slimy, intelligent, knowing, unmerciful, predatory.   Every time I breathed in, they tightened their grip.

Ok , I'm going to die.

I was getting crushed and it was the ego and personality part of me that was gasping for air.   My lungs had nowhere to go, no room, no strength against these beasts. They tightened again and then both their heads were at the level of my eyes - they hissed with repulsion.   I gave in, I surrendered, I had no answers or strength against them......I died.

Boom! For the next hour I was hacking through tunnels, and seeing hosts of light and dark entities, it was too fast, some images from my emotional past presented themselves in gruesome ways too, it was too much, when I could grasp for any *I-ness*, like a drowning child, I wanted it to stop. My human vessel in the large tent, in the field in Glastonbury, all seemed light years and multiple dimensions away – I tried to hold on…..to what, I didn't know……I was sinking in fractals upon fractals.

Forms would appear and melt into other forms, hundreds of images, a roller coaster, flung about, fast, slow, deep, high, I tried to hold on, to get any sort of grip….on anything.   How long had past? Three hours?   Three years? An epoch?

Then it slowed down, there was space – I could see stars, galaxies, and I felt a massive sense of awareness. Some serenity, some awareness, some stability, and a lot of bliss…….

"Are you coming Mark?" I heard.

I looked and two (what I can only describe as) neon-galactic-butterfly-demigod-fairy-angels were either side of me. I felt pure love emanate from each of them – each the same flavour.   We had a connection that we were one, and the forms of ourselves were silly theatre, only for my amusement, and also for theirs. They looked near identical; humanoid, angelic, and their edges were made up of fractals. They would slip into drunk, geometric, pulsing, mega-colour, fractals and then giggle and come back to their slick, godhead-party-girl look…..a costume for sure.

We flew through space with me in-between them. As we sped up I felt love like never before, and the stars and galaxies either side whizzed past, each bursting with the energy of life and galactic dance. It made no sense as each had a just a soft flap of their silky butterfly-like wings to propel them.   It didn't matter, rational had long gone.

"Watch this Mark!" the one to my left said giving me a look that blew a higher dimensions of love into me – as if ten trillion first kisses had been blasted at me from a simple smile.

She uncoiled her elegant, angelic, arm – and rolling down her arm and springing from her fingertips came a universe – and I followed it, I had no choice, and in a split second I followed it from universe > galaxy > solar system > planet > life form, then whizzed back up to continue the flight in-between the two angelic butterfly love beings.

Then the one to my right did the same, and after a while they were just spinning universes out of them near continuously, each created by pure divine love, and each time I followed at impossible speed down to the life forms then back up – in a fraction of a second. But I could feel all the energy in each planet as though I was there for over a year each.   I was in awe, I loved them, I wanted this journey to never end.....I would have given anything for this to be for eternity.

We came to a stop. We were at the edge of infinity, the abyss in Qabalistic terms I guess, and they said they were going to a galactic party (in that moment their faces changed to create some sort of galactic-makeup-tantric-style-party-look).

 "I wanna come....pleeeeaase" – I mumbled out pathetically with humility, backed by massive attachment and clinging.

They each smiled at me with love and knowing, probably making my human vessel back in the large tent quiver and spasm, and I knew at that moment I wasn't ready.

They left me, and danced off into the infinity in front of me and I felt the decrease and leaving of the intense love frequency. They swooped and flew as they had done on our journey, like some sort of galactic butterflies.

"Come back, please....." I called.

A second later I was back in the tunnels again......trying to hold on.......my vessel in the tent writhed and purged, as some other human eyes looked at my vessel with concern and bewilderment.

The End

"Only those that have gone beyond the world can change the world."

Other works by the same author:

Wayki Wayki 2008
Trinity of Wisdom;
        Truth, Philosophy, & Hermetic Alchemical Qabala 2010
The Reemergence of Man 2012

Articles, Blogs, and more @ www.waykiwayki.com

AFTERNOTE

Alone up the mountain, one night I was in the yurt contemplating whether to start this book. I was rummaging through notes I had made over many months, most barely illegible, and started to contemplate the name of the book. *Newrealm, Nurealm, NoRealm*. These and others flew from the pencil into the notepad, onto a page I could barely see as the only light was from a single still candle flame, plus a dancing flicker from a gap in the iron door of the log burner.

Nurielm, *hmm, what can I see, I see something...Ah Uriel, Uriel, the Archangel of the North, Uriel, N-uriel-m*. Then all of a sudden, out of the gradual darkness, a white butterfly came to rest upon the lower part of my index finger as I wrote the word for the first time.

I felt energy, a lot of energy.

As I finished writing the word, the white butterfly flew off gracefully into the nearby darkness. I knew, never to be seen again. The book was to start.